DEAD MAN
FLOATING

Debra Purdy Kong

Enjoy!

Debra Purdy Kong

DEAD MAN FLOATING
Evan Dunstan Mystery #1

www.debrapurdykong.com

FIRST EDITION Paperback

October 15, 2016

Published by Imajin Qwickies®, an imprint of Imajin Books®

www.ImajinQwickies.com

ISBN: 978-1-77223-282-0

Cover designed by Ryan Doan: www.ryandoan.com

Chapter One

Security guard Evan Dunstan pedaled faster. He didn't have to check his watch. He knew he was behind schedule thanks to Jenson Freakin' Morlee, the world's biggest supervisory douche bag. What in holy hell had he done to piss Jenson off this time? Or was the moron so bored that he thought it would be fun to make the bike patroller ride across Southwest Trades & Technology's entire campus just to unlock a damn door for the janitors? The foot patrol guard in this zone could have handled the request. Judging from the radio silence, the newbie hadn't had a busy shift.

Evan raced down the walkway next to the stream that ran along the eastern perimeter of campus. It had rained an hour ago then stopped. But the April night air still felt so damp and heavy that Evan figured the sky would crack open and dump on him any second. Thank god his shift was nearly over.

He'd almost reached the footbridge when a large dark blob in the stream caught his attention. Shit. When would people stop dumping bags of garbage in the damn water? With a new subdivision being built north of campus, a light industrial area to the west, plus six crowded dorms on the premises, the culprit could be anyone. Evan skidded to a stop and frowned. Although floodlights from the engineering building cast some light on the narrow stream, it was too dark to clearly see the bag. Wait a sec. Something was off. What was that white stuff protruding from the bag?

Propping the kickstand, Evan removed the small flashlight attached to his belt then stepped nearer the water. Oh shit! It was a hand! A freakin' hand! And legs! He moved the flashlight up the body until he spotted the grey fringe circling a bald head that glowed like a moon. Evan shivered. Was the guy alive? He wouldn't have to perform CPR, would he? That first-aid course last year didn't go so well after he broke that manikin.

"Hey!" Evan called out. "Can you hear me?"

No response. Sweat broke out on Evan's back. He glanced around for help but no one was around. Where the hell was the foot patrol guy anyway? He was supposed to help monitor water levels whenever it rained. On his knees, Evan extended his arm and touched the wrist. Oh, man. Ice cold. He lifted the man's head out of the water and gasped at the vacant eyes. Scrapes ran across the bulbous forehead and nose. Evan yelped and recoiled, landing on his butt.

The widely despised George Krenn, head of the plumbing department, was about to give him nightmares for the rest of his life. Evan felt the dampness seep through his cargo pants, but he was too busy freaking out to care. Shit. Why hadn't he ignored the blob and kept on riding? Oh, god. This was bad.

Evan spotted a booze bottle on the edge of the bank. Scrambling to his feet, he walked cautiously along the wet grass and then poked the bottle with his toe. Vodka. Krenn's favourite, and it was nearly empty.

So, the asshole had gotten wasted once again. Only this time he lost his balance then fell and drowned in three feet of water. Figured. Krenn was a reckless guy with a God complex.

Evan's shift ended in less than ten minutes. If he reported this, there'd be questions, then cops, then more questions, and report writing. He hated writing reports. Worse, he'd miss his only chance to hook up with Cecelia, the hottest woman he'd ever met in his life. All because of a nasty dip-shit who'd tried to get him fired two weeks ago?

"Oh, hell no."

Evan struggled to his feet and scanned the area again. Still no one in sight. No surprise, he supposed. Evening classes ended over an hour ago and there were only two cars in the parking lot next to engineering. Obviously, no one was in the sports field on the other side of the stream. Maybe the emptiness was a good thing. Even if the newbie found Krenn, Jenson would make the whole team stick around to account for every second of their whereabouts.

"Alpha One to Alpha Two."

Speaking of that ass-wipe...Jenson hadn't seen something, had he? Oh, no. What about the cameras? Camera twenty-one kept tabs on the east entrance to engineering and twenty-two monitored the parking lot. But both could be panned to cover the field and portions of the stream. Evan wiped his hands on his pants then pressed the button on his shoulder mic.

"Go ahead," he replied as calmly as he could.

"Have you locked up engineering yet?"

"En route."

"Change of plans. Head to admin. CFO needs help with the alarm code again. Alpha Three will take care of engineering."

"Ten-four."

Grateful to get away from this horror show, Evan pedalled as fast as his rubbery legs would allow. Why had Krenn been near engineering anyway? The plumbing building was much closer to the west side of campus. Come to think of it, Evan had seen him up here a couple of times over recent weeks, but Krenn wouldn't have appreciated being questioned about it. In fact, most guards had learned to avoid the rude bastard.

Evan stopped the bike. If he didn't calm

down and get it together the CFO would notice that something was wrong. And that could come become a problem. Besides, rules dictated that all requests were supposed to be written in the guard's notebook as soon as they came in.

Evan wiped the sweat from his brow. He tried to keep his hand from shaking as he carefully printed the time of the lockup request. When he was done, his face still felt flushed. Nothing he could do about that, or the sweat trickling down his sides. Taking a deep breath, Evan began pedalling.

At the administration building, he plastered on a smile that was supposed to say, *Everything's cool. No dead bodies around here. None at all.* Chief financial officer Nigel Gardner stood inside the building near the glass doors. As Evan approached, Gardner stepped outside. For an accountant who worked with numbers all day, Gardner sure had a hard time remembering four-digit codes. This code changed a week ago and he still hadn't gotten his act together.

"Sorry, Evan," Gardner said. "I know I'm being stupid, but it's been a long day."

"No worries." Evan swiped his card

through the slot then pressed the digits. Nothing happened.

"You okay, Evan? You look a little jittery."

"Hands are cold. Forgot to bring my gloves." Which was true. He'd left them in the lunchroom after dinner. Jenson wouldn't let him go back to retrieve them. Evan forced himself to concentrate on the number pad. On the second try, the red light went on, locking the door and setting the alarm. "There you go. The code's four, two, six, one."

"Thanks, Evan. I'll try to remember."

While Gardner hurried toward the parking lot, Evan scribbled down the time he set the alarm. Man, he'd be late for shift change. Evan hopped on the bike and listened for mention of the stream on the two-way radio. Each time the radio crackled and a guard reported in, Evan held his breath, terrified that Krenn would be discovered. He'd almost reached HQ when the rain started again.

"Thank you," he murmured to the sky.

Guards would stay inside during a downpour. With luck, Krenn wouldn't be discovered for hours. Evan entered the locker room, where the afternoon guards were already passing radios and keys to the graveyard team. The newbie who should have checked the stream before the shift ended, leaned back in his chair and laughed at some joke. Newbie was either a born actor or he had no clue that a dead guy was floating in his zone.

Evan tossed his notebook, jacket, and utility belt in the locker.

"Why is your butt all wet?" his replacement asked.

"Slid on a wet patch and fell." Evan handed him his keys and radio. "Quiet night. Nothing to report."

"For god's sake, Evan," Jenson said, glaring at him with those pale narrow eyes. "You didn't damage the bike, did you?"

Evan turned away. "It's fine."

Jenson's red hair and beard reminded Evan of a picture he once saw of Vincent Van Gogh, only meaner. Evan had long suspected his short supervisor resented Evan's six-foot, two-inch, broad-shouldered frame. He also believed that Jenson would take Krenn's death hard. Jenson was one of the few people on campus who liked Krenn, but then those two had a lot in common.

Grabbing his street clothes, Evan decided to change in the car off campus. He needed to get out of here before the shit-storm came. His buddy's birthday party was already underway. It was a stroke of luck that his buddy's girlfriend was studying nursing with Cecelia, and that the girls had become friends. Security rules prevented guards from asking students out while on duty. But there was no rule about off duty and off campus action. No way in hell would he let this evening's disaster ruin his chance with the world's most gorgeous woman.

Chapter Two

GET BACK TO HQ. URGENT! Evan stared at Jenson's text, wishing to hell he hadn't read it. Evan had hoped that Krenn's body wouldn't be found this fast. His phone rang earlier, but the party was too loud to bother answering. He recognized the number, though. Dispatch. A second call came from Jenson's cell. Evan hadn't listened to the voice mail. Everyone who'd worked the afternoon three-to-eleven shift had probably been ordered back to campus. Jenson Freakin' Morlee would enjoy interrogating him. Well, screw that. Evan could pretend that he forgot his phone in the car. He just wanted to ignore the Krenn nightmare and focus on good music, food, beer, and above all Cecelia.

Evan shoved the phone in his pocket and watched Cecelia talk to some girls. She looked so hot in that purple tank top and black skirt. Evan held his breath. She was looking at him. They'd been making eye contact and nodding to each other for the past hour. Evan had intended to approach her straight up, but the image of Krenn floating like a baby whale in the black water messed with his confidence. By the time he was ready to make his move, Cecelia was surrounded by a bunch of guys. It kept happening. A couple times, she'd started toward him only to be accosted by some gawking idiot.

Cecelia stepped away from her admirers. She flashed Evan a brilliant smile, then started toward him. She didn't get far when the birthday boy grabbed her by the arm, twirled her around and began dancing. Evan shook his head. His phone vibrated in his pocket. Damn it! Evan looked at the screen, surprised to see that his friend Sully was calling. Sully was Krenn's least favourite plumbing student. Evan headed to the kitchen where it was a little quieter.

"George Krenn is dead!" Sully blurted.

"The cops want to question me. What should I do?"

"Why do they want to question you?"

"Because they think I killed him! I'm in deep shit, man."

"What are you talking about?" Evan shot back. "Krenn got wasted and drowned in the stream. End of story."

"How do you know? I heard that he was only found a half hour ago."

Uh-oh. As much as Evan liked Sully, the guy wasn't good with secrets. "We'll talk later."

"You've been called back to work, haven't you?"

Evan frowned. "How do you know?"

"'Cause I'm here on campus, dude! I've been hearing stuff and if you don't come back it'll make you look bad."

"What stuff? What's going on? And why are you there so late?"

"I was having major problems with a stupid project that's due tomorrow. Listen, there's a rumour that Krenn's death wasn't an accident."

"Seriously?"

"Totally."

The nachos and wings in Evan's

stomach swirled like a washing machine on heavy-duty cycle. "I thought you were shittin' me."

"Not this time. Cops are everywhere," Sully replied. "I'll wait for ya."

He hung up before Evan could ask anything more. Evan chugged the cold beer, but his insides felt as if they were on fire. He couldn't breathe! Evan stepped onto the sundeck and gulped down air. Once again, the rain had stopped. He hoped that any trace of his footprints or bike tires had been washed away from the stream's bank.

Evan turned his back to the railing and spotted Cecelia's bright green eyes looking straight at him. She waved. Oh, god. Attempting a smile, Evan waved back. His heart flipped. His phone pinged.

WHERE ARE YOU? Jenson's text screamed. *IF YOU DON'T CALL RIGHT NOW YOU'RE FIRED!*

Cecelia was almost outside when some guy stepped in front of her and started yammering. For once, Evan was grateful. He needed to think, to act. Hell, he needed to keep his damn job. What should he say to Jenson? Evan really didn't know much. Hadn't seen anyone by the stream. And no one had seen him, unless one of the cameras had picked him up.

Was this why Jenson wanted him back there so badly? The odds of cameras on the stream were remote. Dispatchers were supposed to keep them focused on building entrances and parking lots. The dispatch guards only moved cameras when things were slow, but the evening classes usually kept things busy.

Swallowing hard, Evan dialed. "What's up, Jenson?"

"Were you near the stream tonight?"

Edgy and to the point. "You know that I am every shift."

"Don't be a smart ass. Did you see *anything* in the stream?"

Sweat oozed from every pore. Evan leaned over the railing. "No. Why?"

"George Krenn was found floating near the footbridge." His voice cracked. "Dead."

Evan wished he could say, *Good riddance*. "There are three footbridges. Which one?"

"In front of engineering."

"Shit, man. That's too bad. How'd it happen?"

"Apparent drowning."

Apparent? Was Sully right? Was something else going on?

"The police want to talk to you, so get your ass over here now."

Evan's stomach gurgled. If the cops found out he was there and didn't report it, he could kiss his dream of joining the RCMP or any municipal police force goodbye.

"I don't think I can drive. I'm workin' on my third beer." Sort of. He'd plunked the bottle on the counter before he went outside.

"Have you had any food?" Jenson asked.

"Yeah."

"Then you'll be fine. Now get over here!" He hung up.

Evan lowered his head. His heart pounded.

"Hi, Evan," Cecelia said as she approached. "I've been hoping to talk to you." Her smile faded. "Are you okay? You look kind of upset."

Evan tried to hold the wings at bay. But they were flapping too fast. Oh, hell. He spun around and vomited everything over the railing. Evan heaved three times before he was done. Looking down, he was pretty certain that his dignity was sitting on that lumpy puddle.

"Hey, moron!" someone yelled below. "Spew someplace else!"

"Sorry."

Aware of the laughter and crude remarks about his "epic hurl," Evan wiped his mouth with the back of his hand then rested his head on his forearm. He wanted to catch his breath, to regain what little control he had over his body. But then he remembered Cecelia. Evan looked up. She was gone. Who could blame her? This humiliation would be burned into his memory forever. Evan started down the back steps.

"Evan?" Cecelia said.

He stopped and looked over his shoulder. "You came back." His already flushed face grew warmer.

"Thought you could use these." She handed him several paper towels.

"Thanks." He wiped his mouth. "I'm so sorry. Never did that in front of people before."

"Don't worry about it. That's what beer and parties are for," she replied. "If I let vomit bother me, what kind of nurse would I make?"

"You'll make a great one."

"Thanks." She watched him. "You sure you're okay?"

"Yeah. It wasn't just the beer. I got some bad news and have to go back to campus."

"What happened?"

He hesitated, not knowing how much to tell her. "Someone drowned in Birch Stream."

"Oh, my god." She covered her hand with her mouth. "Who? How?"

"I'll fill you in when I know more. Maybe we can talk tomorrow? I'm working the afternoon shift again."

Cecelia nodded. "I'll look for you."

Sweet relief. "Okay." Evan headed for his car.

Sticking to the speed limit wasn't a problem. He needed time to figure out how to handle the questions that were waiting for him. By the time Evan reached the campus, he still had no strategy. He pulled into parking lot A, the one that guards shared with students, and which was still a five minute walk from HQ. Evan stepped out of the car and began walking until the sight of three patrol cars in front of HQ made him freeze.

"Hey, Five-O," a familiar voice said.

"Your future's here, and it don't look good."

Evan flinched and turned around. Sully was the only person on campus who knew about his career aspirations.

"What the hell does that mean?"

"I overheard a guard say that you were near the stream tonight." Sully watched him. "Did you know about Krenn before your shift ended?"

Oh, shit. Maybe he had been caught on camera. "This isn't the time to get into it, Sully. We'll talk tomorrow, I promise."

Sully stuffed a donut in his mouth. He always ate them whenever he was under stress, which was a lot. Krenn had badgered Sully constantly. Said he was too stupid and clumsy to be a decent plumber. Evan had gotten to know Sully because of the many times Sully had to stay after his evening class to finish a project. Sully always offered donuts to any guard who had to come by and lock up after him.

"You're not their main suspect," Sully mumbled through sugary lips. "I am."

"What? Why?"

"The cop already knew that I worked late tonight, and that Krenn threatened to fail me if I didn't finish the assignment by tomorrow."

"Any idea who told him?"

"Could be anyone. Krenn was loud enough for most of the students to hear. Everyone knows that I was number one on his shit list."

"It was a long list, and I was up there too," Evan replied. "Besides, you don't know for certain that he was murdered."

Sully chewed for a few more seconds. "Dude, he's with IHIT."

"Oh, no."

When murders happened in smaller BC municipalities, local police forces often worked with the Integrated Homicide Investigation Team. Pooled resources saved time and money. But why were they already here? What had they discovered? More to the point, Evan wondered what the hell he'd missed. He'd been too freaked out to take a close look at Krenn's body.

"What did the cop ask?" Evan said.

"If I got along with Krenn, if he had problems with anyone on campus."

"What'd you say?"

"What *could* I say? It would have taken half the night to name everyone who had problems with the jerk. So, I only said that he gave staff and students a hard time now and then." Sully finished the donut. "When the cop pushed for more, I told him that Krenn was a racist bully, which everyone knows anyhow."

True. Krenn had despised all visible minorities but he especially hated Asians. Seeing as how Sully was a Vietnamese immigrant, he never stood a chance.

"Wonder what the coroner will find," Sully murmured.

Evan stared at HQ, half expecting Jenson to charge out and drag him inside. "What time did Krenn leave the building tonight?"

"A few minutes after class ended at eight-thirty. I needed some food, so I took a break a little after at nine and called security to lock up. Vlad came over about five minutes later. His replacement let me back in an hour after that."

Evan remembered hearing the lockup request over the radio. Vladimir Bondarenko liked patrolling the trades zone, seeing as how the buildings had few stairs.

"My timeline sucks, Evan. Doubt anyone will remember me at the McDonald's drive-thru window." Sully stared at the donut. "If I'm arrested and kicked out of school, Dad will kill me."

According to Sully, his father was an angry, hardworking baker who lashed out when enraged. He expected Sully to learn a better-paying skill. Krenn had given Sully such lousy grades after the first year that Sully was now on academic probation.

"If things go bad for me, I might as well be dead!" Sully scrunched the donut bag.

"Relax, Sully. McDonald's probably has security cameras to give you an alibi."

"What if they're not working properly?"

"They still need evidence to arrest you, which they won't find, right?" Even though Sully nodded, Evan noticed that he couldn't quite meet his gaze. "Khalid Chourki had issues with Krenn, especially after Krenn took over his evening class. Won't the cops be taking a close look at him and the other plumbing instructors? Is Chourki here?"

"I haven't seen him, and he never came by while Krenn was teaching," Sully replied. "I think Krenn liked hanging around at night. That way he could skulk around campus with no one watching. God knows what he got up to."

"If they haven't already, they might call

Chourki in soon."

Evan looked at HQ and sighed. It was one of the smaller buildings on campus. A drab single-storey concrete box that was home to the security director, administrative personnel, the communications centre and guards. A tiny storage shed in back held bicycles, traffic cones and other tools of the trade.

"Better get this over with," Evan muttered.

"Let me know what they say," Sully said.

As Evan headed toward the building, Vladimir stepped outside HQ. Vlad was as tall as Evan but three times as wide. The Ukrainian's perpetually stern expression kept students in line. Few people knew that he was actually a decent guy, which was how Vlad liked to keep things.

"Hey," Evan said. "Did the cops question you about George Krenn?"

Vlad nodded and stepped closer to Evan. "Trust no one," he murmured in his heavy accent. "Things not what they seem."

"What do you mean?" Evan waited, but Vlad started for the parking lot. "Was Krenn murdered?"

Vlad stomped back to him. "Don't say it out loud. There's enough trouble tonight. Enemies crawling out of fuckin' walls and blaming others."

"Blaming for what? Krenn's death?" Vlad's stony expression told Evan that he wouldn't get an answer. "Sully's worried that they think he killed Krenn."

Vlad's pale eyes glinted in the darkness. "We should all be worried. Say nothing."

Vlad knew something, but did he honestly think that silence would work? Cops and supervisors had a way of finding things out. Colleagues ratted on one another all the time, thinking it would help them get ahead or gain a few privileges. Maybe Vlad was right to trust no one.

Chapter Three

Taking a deep breath, Evan stepped through HQ's public entrance. The frazzled looking dispatcher on the phone barely glanced at him. The other dispatcher turned away from the CCTV footage she was reviewing and gaped at Evan with a strange mix of puzzlement and wariness.

"Okeyo's waiting for you in the conference room," she said.

Not wanting to appear anxious, Evan strolled down the hallway. He should have known that Okeyo Abasi would be here. As director of security, Okeyo dealt with every serious issue. Okeyo was a no-nonsense man and the only one Jenson Morlee answered to, and therefore both feared and hated.

Guards had heard the two of them argue many times. As hard as Jenson tried to hide it, his racism and resentment peeked through when he was pissed about something.

The Kenyan-born Okeyo was six-foot three, astute, and better educated than Jenson. Okeyo knew how to put Jenson in his place. No doubt, Jenson wished him gone, preferably through disgrace from firing, but that wouldn't happen. Okeyo's reputation as an honest, hardworking man was solid.

The moment Evan entered the conference room, Okeyo and another man stopped talking. Even if the room had been full of people, Evan would have known that this was the cop. He sat straight and still, his laser stare unrelenting.

The cop and Okeyo sat at one end of the long oak table. Okeyo's eyes were bloodshot. The thin scar that ran from his cheekbone to his chin twitched. Evan had only seen that happen when Okeyo was stressed, but why wouldn't he be? The only good thing about this situation was that he and Okeyo got along well.

"Hello, Evan," Okeyo said in an unnervingly calm voice. "Have a seat." He nodded toward the chair directly across from the cop.

Evan's heart raced. He pulled the chair out so hard that it nearly toppled. So much for a cool demeanour. As he sat, the chair wobbled. He shifted slowly in the cracked plastic seat, afraid that another careless gesture would throw him off balance. Both men had coffee mugs in front of them. Evan wished he had a coffee. He ran his hand through his hair. Before the party, it had been neatly pulled back from his forehead. Now it was probably a dishevelled mess. And his breath stank to holy hell.

"This is Corporal Renton," Okeyo said, turning to the cop. "Evan Dunstan is our bike patroller and one of our most reliable employees. He's also worked as a supervisor on some Sunday shifts. He has the potential to move quickly up the ranks."

Evan gave Okeyo an appreciative nod. Or was the endorsement supposed to make him feel comfortable, let his guard down? Evan tried not to wither under Renton's stare. Although the guy had few lines on his long angular face, his temples were greying.

"I understand that Jenson told you what happened tonight," Okeyo said.

"Yes."

"Your duties have been described to the corporal." Okeyo paused. "We perused your notebook and know where you patrolled tonight."

Evan expected this. How many times had he told trainees that guards weren't allowed to take notebooks home, and that supervisors required everyone's locker combination? The periodic checks for accurate and detailed notes were important, especially if a guard had to rely on those notes in court one day. Occasionally, information was needed instantly, like tonight.

"Corporal Renton has more questions. I want you to answer truthfully, understand?" Okeyo's subdued tone didn't match the intensity in his eyes.

"Yes. But can I ask two questions first?"

Okeyo and Renton exchanged glances.

"What do you want to know?" Renton said.

Evan's jaw clenched. He ordered himself to relax. "Someone just told me that Mr. Krenn was murdered. Is it true?"

"We prefer to wait for the autopsy results before we say anything," Renton replied.

Then he either didn't know how Krenn died or didn't want the guards to know yet.

"Your second question?" Okeyo asked.

It was risky, but Evan couldn't help himself. "Did the CCTV cameras show Mr. Krenn by the stream?"

Okeyo and Renton again glanced at each other.

"Do you think they will?" Okeyo asked.

"I don't know."

"You sound a little concerned," Renton said.

Evan wished he had something to look at besides their faces and the plain beige walls. "It's just that I've never had to deal with a workplace fatality before."

Both men remained silent, their faces impassive. Renton reached for one of a half dozen black notebooks in front of him. He flipped to the last page and studied it for what felt like an unnecessarily long time.

At last, he looked at Evan, his expression in full scrutiny mode. "There's no reference to your activities between 10:15 p.m. when you were asked to lock up the engineering building and 10:30, when you were sent to activate the alarm at administration. What did you do during that time?"

Evan's brain froze. What the hell was he supposed to say? That he found and then abandoned a dead guy in Birch Stream? He fidgeted in the wobbly chair, hoping he'd fall over, hit his head, and pass out.

"I don't remember every minute," Evan mumbled. "I've been to a party. Had a couple beers."

Okeyo frowned. Evan had a horrible feeling that these two knew more than they were letting on.

"What *do* you remember?" Renton asked.

Oh, god. There was no getting around this. He gnawed on his lower lip.

"Evan?" Okeyo said, his tone formidable.

"Okay. Look," he replied. "This is what I know."

Evan babbled about glimpsing what he thought was a garbage bag until he realized it was Krenn. He described the white blobs, lifting Krenn's head, the shock and fear, and then spotting the vodka bottle. By the time Evan finished speaking he was exhausted and dripping sweat onto the table. Vlad's warning flashed through his brain. Had confessing been a huge mistake? He couldn't tell a damn thing from Okeyo's blank expression. Renton was busy scribbling notes.

"Why didn't you report this, Evan?" Okeyo asked.

That was the million-dollar question. The one that would have the greatest consequence. Disciplinary measures would be coming. A suspension. Maybe he'd be fired. Evan's stomach gurgled. He wiped the drops from the table with his sleeve.

"There was nothing I could do for Mr. Krenn," Evan murmured. "My shift was almost over and there was the party…a girl I'd been dying to ask out. Tonight was my only chance." His voice trailed away.

"You realize you made a terrible decision, don't you?" Okeyo said.

"Yeah," he mumbled. "But I was also afraid that Jenson would twist the truth and find a reason to suspend, or even fire me."

Okeyo nodded. "He probably would have."

"If you were that worried, why didn't you contact Mr. Abasi directly?" Renton asked.

"It was late, he was off duty, and I didn't know anything useful," Evan replied. "There was no sign of violence. No one was around."

From underneath the notebooks, Renton produced a larger sheet. Evan recognized a map of the campus.

"Birch Stream runs down the east side of the campus," Renton said, placing his finger on the engineering building. "I gather there's not much around there. Just a playing field, then a wooded area, and then the marsh, which I'm told is fenced off to protect nesting grounds."

"That's right."

"So, why would you take that route to lock up engineering?"

"Because it's also my job, along with the guard who patrols that zone, to monitor the stream's water levels whenever it rains," Evan replied. "The stream's not wide, and is pretty shallow in places. Flooding's been a problem for engineering many times."

Renton nodded. "I'm told that the bottom's rocky in some spots."

"It is. And because the stream's out of the way it's used as a dumping ground. I usually ride by it on my way to engineering."

"Do you get a lot of garbage dumped there?"

"More than we should, yeah."

Renton again looked at the map. "Why would Mr. Krenn be in that area when the plumbing building is near the southwest corner of campus?"

"I don't know. But I and other guards have seen him wandering around campus at night, often with a bottle in his hand. Plenty of people on campus knew about Mr. Krenn's drinking problem since his wife and kids left him." Renton's laser stare returned, so Evan quickly added, "Mr. Krenn was quite vocal about his personal problems when he was drunk, especially around plumbing instructors and students."

Renton flipped a page in his notebook. "Would one of those students be Mr. Sinh La, also known as Sully?"

Uh-oh. "I think so. Yes."

"I've heard from more than one source that you and he are good friends."

The rat bastard co-workers were at it again. "Yes."

"Has Mr. Sinh La ever complained to you about Mr. Krenn's treatment of him?"

"A number of students have." Evan cleared his throat. "I don't mean to be disrespectful, but since you want the truth, it's common knowledge that Mr. Krenn didn't treat staff and students too well."

Renton kept his gaze on him. "Is it true that Mr. Krenn often singled out Mr. Sinh La?" Renton asked. "Forced him to stay late to finish assignments?"

"Yes."

Renton turned to another page. "I understand that you had a run-in with Mr. Krenn two weeks ago."

Evan's chair wobbled. Had Okeyo told him, or was it someone else? "Mr. Krenn went ballistic when I started to lock up his office one night. He usually does it, but that night the door was unlocked and the lights were off. I had no idea he was sitting in the dark." Evan hesitated. "He said that his desk lamp was on and that I should have noticed it if I was doing my job properly. But I swear it was off."

"I stand by Evan on this," Okeyo said. "George Krenn liked to cause my team trouble. I also have numerous documented complaints from staff and students who were manipulated and bullied through silly pranks and other nonsense."

"Was he ever disciplined?" Renton asked.

"I wrote a report to the vice president last month," Okeyo replied. "He's been interviewing staff and students, and was planning to interview the guards soon."

This was news to Evan. Too bad it hadn't happened earlier.

Renton turned to Evan. "That's all for now. Thank you for coming in."

He was about to say, "No problem." But Renton would probably see through the lie.

Once Evan cleared HQ, he began to jog. He needed to get out of here before Renton decided he had more questions. As it stood, Evan figured he'd probably blown any chance of a career with an integrated law enforcement team. Maybe he'd have to stay a freakin' guard forever. It wasn't fair that a jerk like Krenn could cost him his dream job. By the time Evan reached his car he was starting to hyperventilate.

"What did the cop say?" Sully asked from behind.

Evan recoiled as if he'd been struck. "Shit, Sully!" He gasped for air.

Sully handed him a paper bag. "The

donuts are gone. Breathe into that. It helps.'

Evan waved it away. "I'll be fine." He took a slow, calming breath. "Why are you still here?"

Sully sighed. "Wanted to know if my name came up."

Revealing too much would make him paranoid. Judging from the way Sully fidgeted, he was already on an edgy sugar high.

"Renton only asked if you knew about Krenn's drinking and personal problems." He took another deep breath. "I told him that tons of people knew."

Sully scrunched the empty bag. "Everyone's gonna think I did it."

"Or me." Evan paused. "When the full story comes out."

"Why you?"

"Because of what I did, or didn't do, tonight."

Sully's mouth fell open. "What are you talking about?

After Evan again described how he found Krenn, his energy was almost drained.

"Wow," Sully murmured. "You might need a lawyer, dude."

This from the prime suspect. Evan tilted

his head back and looked at the starless sky. Could this night get any worse?

"But I didn't kill Krenn. It's not even clear that the guy was murdered."

"It will be, which means the killer needs a scapegoat. Who better than one of us?" Sully shook his head. "The cops might think we're in on it together."

"Renton's aware of Krenn's many enemies. Apparently, Okeyo has a file full of complaints about him."

"Then it's a good thing I told him about Chourki's battles with Krenn."

Evan nodded. Khalid Chourki had been a sessional instructor for ten years. Plenty of students and instructors had overheard arguments between him and Krenn. When a full-time plumbing instructor retired a few weeks back, Chourki applied for the position. Rumour was that Krenn had been trying to sabotage the native Moroccan's efforts. Taking over Chourki's evening class had been just been one of his tactics.

"I might have been wrong about not seeing Chourki tonight," Sully murmured.

"What?"

"Well, it's kind of weird, but I thought I saw him leave the building right after Krenn did. I was working at the other end, though, and can't say for sure." Sully's eyebrows rose and his round face became animated. "What if Chourki followed him?"

"The timing's interesting," Evan remarked. "I don't think Krenn had been in the water long before I found him."

"We should do our own investigating."

Evan snorted. "Sure, Sully."

"Look, you wanna be a cop and you've got mad computer skills, plus access to places most of us don't have."

"Which I can't enter without a good reason."

"Come on, Evan. Solving the crime could fast-track you into the RCMP. Maybe land you a pay raise or the attention of that pretty nursing student."

Evan cringed. Could he redeem himself with Cecelia?

"At the very least you could prove that we didn't do it."

If Krenn truly had been murdered, then Sully was right. Someone could try to set them up. Still..."Questioning people and rooting out suspects could cause a huge backlash."

"We can't be scapegoats," Sully argued.

"We'll do it on the down-low. I'll be your sidekick. Asian guys are always sidekicks, right? You'll be da man, the one in charge, bro. You got to think like a cop now."

"Sully, have you ever thought about watching Masterpiece Theatre?"

"Tried it. But this homeboy don't like all that posh talk. So, come on, Five-O. Save our butts."

Just what he needed. A Vietnamese, crime-solving homeboy. "Let's wait until there's confirmation of a homicide before we start asking questions, okay?"

"Sure thing, boss. But we won't have to wait long," Sully said. "'Cause I'm telling ya right now. This was murder."

Chapter Four

Evan bolted upright in bed, covered in sweat, his head pounding. In the nightmare, Krenn's body-less face peered at him from the water, his eyes blinking, mouth opening and closing like a fish. Water streamed over his fat lips as he'd said, '*You're in for it now*.'

Evan stripped off his PJs. Shivering, he grabbed underwear from the drawer. The only problem with living in the family's detached garage was the lack of heating. His dad saw no reason to waste money on electrical heaters in April. When Gran came to live with them, Evan begged his parents to let him move in here to avoid sharing a room with his obnoxious brother. Seeing as how it was the previous owner's workshop, the space came with a tiny bathroom, built-in counters, drawers and electrical outlets. Evan had added a bar fridge, microwave, hotplate and furniture. All the comforts of home mostly, until the living room wall began to rise.

"Shit!" Why wouldn't Dad let him keep all the remotes? Evan had only forgotten his keys a couple of times.

He'd barely gotten his briefs on when Gran and her two friends stood there, grinning.

"I see London, I see France, I see Evvy's underpants!" she sang.

Her friends hooted with laughter. Evan's face reddened, but they didn't notice. The old crones weren't looking in that direction. He grabbed his jeans.

"Evvy, you remember my friends, Flo and Agnes, don't ya? They just got back from Arizona."

"It was hot there," Agnes said, winking at him. "Real hot."

Totally grossed out by the wrinkled pixie, Evan turned away. He hopped from one foot to the other while he put the jeans on. He banged his elbow against the bureau.

"Ow!"

More laughter. Evan groaned. Yeah, freakin' hilarious.

"Nice three-pack," Flo snickered.

"Evvy's working hard," Gran replied defensively. "He's got a bench press in the corner. Come see."

Zipping up, Evan felt like a guppy in a fish bowl. "Do you remember me asking you to use the side door, Gran?"

"Sorry, Evvy. But I wanted to show the girls that garages aren't just for cars." She gave him one of her not-so-innocent smiles. "Anyhow, since it's almost noon I thought you'd be up and dressed by now."

"It's that late?"

Once Evan put on his T-shirt, the old ladies turned their attention to the furniture and the rug on the laminate floor he'd laid himself.

"You're a great interior decorator," Flo remarked. "You should come and do my house."

"Evvy's not interested in interior design," Gran said. "He's going to be a police officer."

Evan's phone pinged. *Come to campus ASAP. Have info on Vlad & Chourki,* Sully texted. Evan sighed. What happened to waiting for the official cause of death before they started snooping around? Interesting that Vlad's name came up, though. Evan had planned to find out what he meant by things not being what they seemed. Vlad was on the day shift right now. Might as well go to the campus early and see if the grouchy Ukrainian would talk to him.

Forty minutes later, Evan cruised by *Parking Lot B* next to engineering to see if the cops were still around. They were. Most of the lot had been cordoned off, allowing only two rows of parked vehicles. Evan stopped to study two men by the stream. One was in hip waders and peering at something in his hand.

Evan removed a small pair of binoculars from the glove box. They came in handy when observing suspicious activity from a distance, which thankfully didn't happen often. The guy in hip waders was showing a phone to his colleague.

Evan drove to *Parking Lot A*, then stepped out of the car. Glancing at HQ, he spotted Corporal Renton talking to a constable and a man in a suit. Curious, Evan moved as close as he dared before retreating to the threshold of a nearby building. He kept the entrance partially open to watch Renton. Too bad he couldn't hear what was being said. Renton started toward HQ's entrance, then stopped and called out, "See if she reported her phone missing."

Probably the one the other cops were studying. They must have found it in the water. Evan doubted that all these officers would still be here over an accidental drowning. Shit. This really was murder.

Renton headed inside HQ. Evan took off in the opposite direction. Halfway across campus, he found the plumbing students eating lunch at a picnic table near their building.

"Evan!" Sully jumped up from the table.

As heads turned, Evan realized that he should have told Sully to meet him some place more private. As Sully jogged toward him, he dropped a donut on the ground, then picked it up.

Evan cringed. "You aren't going eat that, are you?"

Sully brushed the powdered donut with his fingertips. "Where I come from, you don't waste food."

Concerned about cameras and patrolling

guards, Evan said, "Let's go where we can't be seen or heard."

They walked past the plumbing building, turned the corner and stopped. A cracked concrete walkway and narrow strip of grass separated this building from the automotive compound.

"How's everyone taking the news about Krenn?" Evan asked.

"Like they just got the best Christmas present ever." Sully bit into the donut.

"What did you want to tell me about Vlad and Chourki?"

Sully chewed a few moments. "I overheard Chourki talking about him to that cop-in-a-suit."

"How'd you manage that?"

"Got here early. My stomach's been funky so I was in the can before classes started." Sully swallowed the food. "Chourki's office is right across from the bathrooms. Turns out that Krenn caught Vlad helping himself to Krenn's vodka stash. Krenn threatened to have Vlad fired."

"Whoa." Drinking on the job was grounds for dismissal. "When did that happen?"

"Don't know, but it looks like your co-worker had reason to kill the guy." Sully leaned against the brick wall. "Vlad's got a family to support, right?"

"Yeah." Two ex-wives and twin daughters from his current marriage.

"What if he knocked Krenn out then dumped him in the stream?"

Evan didn't want to believe it, but if Krenn threatened Vlad, then anything was possible. Vlad had a hell of a temper.

"Krenn was also mixed up with some woman on campus," Sully added.

"You're joking. The guy was butt ugly. Who would be desperate enough to hook up with him?"

"I heard the name Stadler mentioned, but have no idea who she is."

Evan knew. Veronica Stadler was an evening instructor. The image of a middle-aged blonde with a big dog sprang to mind. Stadler always left the beast in her office while she taught. The dog barked and growled whenever someone knocked on the door. There'd been complaints.

"Wonder if she taught last night," Evan murmured.

"You know who she is?"

"An engineering instructor."

Sully's eyes widened in delight. "Maybe that's why Krenn was near the building last night. Better start investigating, Five-O."

"Are you two playing detective now?"

Evan spun around to find Khalid Chourki standing behind them.

Chapter Five

"I'm just the sidekick!" The colour drained from Sully's face.

Despite the bloodshot eyes and more lines than usual, Chourki grinned. "Of course you are."

Evan couldn't take his gaze off the bright orange tips on Chourki's black curls.

"You like my new look?" Chourki asked him.

"I, uh, well, it's unique."

"Diplomatic. A good quality for an amateur detective," Chourki said, looking at Evan. "My daughter plans to become a beautician. I am her latest guinea pig." He sighed. "You should see what she did to our white Persian cat."

Sully started to laugh, but Chourki's stare cut him off.

"Speaking of things going horribly wrong," Chourki said, "do you honestly think that you can find Krenn's killer?"

"Murder's not been established," Evan replied.

"Oh, he was murdered all right." Chourki lit a cigarette, then inhaled deeply. He tilted his head back and blew smoke in the air.

"Has the autopsy been done?" Evan asked.

"Not that I heard." Chourki's expression became grim. "But if ever a man deserved to be murdered, it was George Krenn."

Evan and Sully exchanged glances.

"We didn't kill him!" Sully blurted.

"I believe you. But you must admit that you had good reason for wanting him dead. Many people did." Chourki folded his arms over his chest. He was painfully thin for a guy in his forties. "I was one of them. And for the record, I didn't drown that pathetic fool. But the police seem interested in me and you two. I think the killer wants them to be."

Evan stared at Chourki. "Are you sure

they're interested in us?"

Chourki's thick mustache twitched. "Corporal Renton asked me how you two got along with Krenn. If there were arguments."

Sully looked worried. "What did you tell him?"

"That Krenn argued with everyone." Chourki studied his cigarette. "Renton already knew about altercations with the big Ukrainian guard. The police are interested in him as well." Chourki turned to Evan. "Maybe you should use those diplomatic skills to prove your innocence. We must do what is necessary to protect ourselves, agreed?"

"Totally," Sully replied.

Evan gave a brief nod, but Chourki worried him. What if he had killed Krenn? Judging from all the kid pictures Evan had seen on Chourki's desk, the man had a large family to support. With Krenn gone, Chourki could apply for his job. The salary would be a hell of a lot better. Did he have an alibi?

"If we're going to investigate," Sully said, "can you tell us if Krenn was involved with Veronica Stadler?"

"He was, but not in the way you think." Chourki looked up and down the walkway. "Last night, I was in my office, catching up on paperwork."

"What time was that?" Evan asked.

"From 7:30 until a little after 8:30." Chourki flicked ashes onto the ground.

"I was there," Sully said. "Saw you leave right after Krenn did. Were you following him?"

Chourki seemed to be assessing Sully, as if trying to decide how much he should say. "That was the plan until my daughter called and begged me to be her model for a class assignment. After the cat incident, her sisters and mother wouldn't let her near their hair." He took a drag on his cigarette.

"So, you spent the rest of the evening at home?" Sully asked.

Chourki gave him a blank stare. "Did you see orange in my hair last night?"

"No."

"It took her quite some time to achieve this look," he said. "I'm sure the corporal thinks that I could have killed Krenn, then rushed home to have my hair turned into this clown's wig. But he doesn't understand my daughter's slow, methodical approach to hair transformation."

Evan did. Gran used to be a hairdresser. It took her forever to do his mom's hair. "How was Krenn involved with Veronica Stadler?"

"I overheard him say that he'd swing by engineering to pick up the money. He used her first name which I found in the campus directory. There's only one Veronica listed in the engineering department, and I'm convinced that Krenn was blackmailing her over something."

"We'd need more evidence than a phone call," Evan said.

Chourki studied him. "You have a knack for police work."

And Evan was thinking like a cop right now. A guilty man would do his best to throw suspicion on others.

"Given that Corporal Renton already knew how much Krenn and I hated each other, my credibility is questionable. But I'll tell you what I told the corporal." Chourki paused. "I've overheard Krenn demand money from others. There has to be physical evidence on this campus somewhere."

"Why not keep it at home or in a safe-deposit box?" Evan asked.

"Because George Krenn was the type of man who'd enjoy throwing it in his victims' faces," Chourki answered. "I'm guessing that he could produce photos, documentation, or perhaps a video recording whenever victims needed reminding of their indiscretions."

"What about his laptop?" Sully asked.

"The police confiscated it, so let's hope they'll find something," Chourki replied. "But part of Krenn was old school. I'm guessing that he hid physical proof near his office."

"In this building?" Sully asked, tapping the wall.

"Yes." Chourki checked his watch. "Class starts in five minutes." He looked at Sully. "Be on time."

As Chourki disappeared around the corner, Sully whispered, "Think Chourki did it? He had motive. Maybe opportunity, despite the hair thing. We should search his office."

"Yeah, but he might not have been the only one with motive and opportunity." Evan thought of Veronica Stadler...and Vlad.

"So, we're going to search for the killer,

right?" Sully asked.

"It's risky. If I'm caught meddling in a homicide investigation, I might as well flush a law enforcement career down the toilet."

"And if we're framed for murder we could wind up in jail. That won't help your career prospects either, dude." Sully wiped his hands on his coveralls. "Remember what Chourki said about Renton's interest in us."

Evan hesitated. It wouldn't take much for his reputation to be trashed. Clearly, someone had already said something to Renton. "All right. Let's do it."

"Excellent. So, what's next, Five-O?"

Evan stared at the grimy windows of the automotive building. "I need to look up Veronica Stadler's teaching schedule and office hours." Since instructors posted schedules on their doors, it would be easy to find.

"You're good with computers. You could hack into her emails. See if there's anything about blackmail."

"I'm not going to do anything illegal, Sully." Unless he had no other option.

"Searching the plumbing building isn't illegal."

"Renton would see it as meddling."

"Then let's not get caught."

"The other problem is Jenson. If he's sending me on errands every five minutes, I won't have time."

"Let's see how it plays out. I've got to go." Sully hurried around the corner and disappeared.

Evan had to admit that the mechanical room would be worth checking out. Those rooms contained fire and electrical panels, which was one reason they were kept locked. As department head, Krenn would have had a key. Instructors should have keys as well, though.

Evan strolled to the front of the building, then down the main road, hoping to find Vlad. To his amazement, he spotted Cecelia heading this way. She was focused on her phone, but when she looked up she smiled. Evan's heart thumped. He removed his sunglasses and grinned like an idiot, but he couldn't stop himself. He was still blown away by a chance encounter with her three weeks ago. Best move he ever made was offering to help her carry those three coffees through the cafeteria. They'd talked. She'd said she hoped to see him again. He'd made sure she had several times since then.

"You're here early," Cecelia said. "Don't you usually start at three?"

"Yes, but I wanted to see a friend before work." He tried not to gape at her tight red sweater. "I'm surprised to see you at this end of campus."

"I had lunch with a girlfriend who's studying carpentry." Cecelia looked around. "Besides, there's more trees and green space here." She turned to him. "Feeling better today?"

Evan cringed. "Yeah. Listen, I want to apologize again."

"It's okay." Cecelia's expression became solemn. "Was the bad news was about the death of that plumbing teacher, George Krenn?"

"You heard?"

"The whole campus is talking about it." She paused. "There's a rumour that it might not have been accidental. So, what happened?"

"The police won't say until the autopsy's done." Evan stared into gorgeous green eyes. "But I'm the one who found him, and I didn't see any sign of violence."

"Oh, Evan! I heard that a guard discovered the body but I never dreamed it was you. I mean, you were at the party and everything." Cecelia's brow furrowed. "Come to think of it, you did seem a little on edge."

"A little? I was totally freaked out, mostly because of what I didn't do last night." Since people would find out anyway, it was better if he told her now. After Evan explained why he didn't report finding Krenn, Cecelia's sympathetic expression filled him with relief. "I know this sounds selfish," he said, "but spending time with you was more important than writing a report about an old boozer who didn't treat people very well."

"Trust me, I understand," Cecelia replied. "Krenn had a nasty reputation among nursing students. We saw the way he leered at us and heard the disgusting remarks."

Evan grimaced. "I should have realized that his pathetic behaviour had reached your end of campus. Sorry you had to go through that. I wish you'd told me."

"What could you have done? We heard that Krenn wielded a lot of power on campus." Cecelia touched his arm. "I've got to get to class. But maybe we could have coffee soon?"

"I'd like that."

"I'll give you my number."

Evan carefully pressed each digit into his phone so he wouldn't make a mistake. As Cecelia left, he watched her long hair gently sway as she moved. He'd call soon. Maybe take her to a movie. He'd been tempted to ask right then and there but was afraid he'd come across as too eager and desperate.

Evan sat at a nearby picnic table and watched the road. Assuming that George Krenn had been murdered, Evan tapped the notes icon on his phone, then typed the names of primary suspects: Khalid Chourki, Veronica Stadler, and—although he hated to do it—Vlad and Sully. No one was above suspicion.

Sully was one of the most passive guys Evan knew, yet Krenn had been more than capable of pushing people to the breaking point. What if Sully snapped last night? Did the guy want to investigate to gain inside knowledge? Was he looking for something incriminating against himself? A letter recommending his expulsion would certainly qualify.

"What are you doing here?" Vlad asked.

Evan looked up, startled. He'd been too busy staring at his list and thinking about Sully to watch for the big guy. "I wanted to talk to you away from HQ."

Vlad frowned. "What for?"

"I heard something about you, and thought you could use a heads up."

Vlad crossed his arms and waited. Even in daylight, his size and defiant stance could make anyone feel threatened. After Evan repeated what he'd heard about the stolen vodka, Vlad's shoulders rounded and the spark in his eyes dimmed.

"Didn't know that Chourki found out." He plunked down on the bench. "I need this job."

Vlad didn't talk much about his past, but he once muttered something about a failed janitorial business. There was another story about him getting fired from a school bus driving job after a nasty incident involving chow mein noodles and a pair of chopsticks. Vlad simply wasn't a people person, which was why he preferred evening and graveyard shifts. Jenson put him on days at least twice a week to make Vlad's life miserable.

"Last night you said that things aren't

what they seem," Evan said. "I need to know what you meant."

Slowly Vlad looked up. "It means Krenn was murdered. Asshole had many enemies."

"How can you know that until the autopsy's done?"

"It is finished. Was on coffee break and heard cop on the phone. Said date rape drug was in vodka bottle. They think killer kept Krenn's head under water." Vlad grunted. "Someone did STT big favour."

"Except that the killer could try to blame one of us," Evan said. "Any thoughts about who did it?"

Vlad snorted. "Too many people to guess."

True. "Can you prove you weren't near that part of the stream last night?"

He grimaced. "I patrolled big empty buildings. Maybe mice and rats will vouch for me."

"If Krenn had gone to Okeyo about you, he would have let you go by now. So, why didn't he?"

Vlad exhaled slowly. "He couldn't."

"Why's that?"

A group of students wandered past them, laughing and joking.

"I found mangled sheet in his shredder." Vlad turned to Evan. "Paper said, *I know what you did* in big letters. Underneath, it said to pay five hundred dollars."

"Whoa. Was there a date or name on the note?"

"No. But I found another version of same note," Vlad replied, "demanding master key to campus."

"Holy shit." A master key could have gained Krenn entry to a lot of labs and offices. "Did you see Krenn last night?"

Vlad stared at him so long that Evan wondered if he'd offended the big guy. "No. Since showing him partly shredded notes last month, he stayed out of my way." Vlad got to his feet. "Be careful. Plenty of backstabbing bastards around here." With that, he continued down the road.

Chapter Six

"Dunstan, you should have been here ten minutes ago."

Jenson Morlee lifted his chin in a lame attempt to appear taller, but it only made his pointy nose look longer. Pale blue eyes glared at Evan with disdain.

"Sorry," Evan replied. "Lost track of time."

After his chat with Vlad, Evan had hurried back to his car to retrieve his laptop. Hacking into emails wasn't hard. STT didn't have decent encryption software and Krenn's passwords were easy to crack. The bastard was also lazy about emptying digital trash. Evan had found what appeared to be a practise blackmail note with three typos. In this case, Krenn wanted a thousand bucks from an unknown individual. The email address hadn't been typed in.

"You'll be on day shifts this week, starting tomorrow," Jenson said.

"Saturday? But that'll make six days in a row."

"You'll get Sunday and Monday off. Deal with it."

There was no point asking why Jenson had changed the schedule. The douche bag never explained his decisions to underlings. It also meant that Evan would have to be here by 7:00 a.m. tomorrow. Since this shift wouldn't end until eleven, the eight-hour turnaround would suck big time.

It wasn't all bad, though. If he patrolled near the dorms maybe he'd see Cecelia. And Jenson never worked weekends, so the moron wouldn't be breathing down his neck.

The other upside was that there might be time to start a little investigating, which reminded him of something. "Hey, Jenson, did any female instructors file a harassment complaint against George Krenn this year?"

The co-workers stopped chatting.

Jenson's brows knitted together. "Why is that your concern?"

"I heard something about him and a woman from engineering. Just wondered if she filed a report or if anyone checked it out." It had occurred to Evan that Veronica Stadler might have tried to seek help in squashing a blackmail attempt.

"Who's spreading stories?"

Whenever Jenson wanted to avoid a question, he asked another question. As site supervisor, he could have buried the paperwork without having to destroy it. Destroying any complaint was grounds for instant dismissal. If Veronica Stadler wanted to know what had been done about the matter, missing paperwork would cause supervisors huge problems.

"Gossip's been flying everywhere," Evan said. "You must have heard things."

"I don't listen to that shit." He glared at the guards. "Neither should any of you." He turned back to Evan. "And stay out of other peoples' business."

A guard called Jenson on his two-way radio and asked him to come to the admin building right away.

Jenson swore under his breath as he pressed the button down. "What for?"

"VP wants to speak with the person in

charge and Okeyo's not here."

Jenson swore under his breath. "Ten-four. En route."

Swearing, he pulled on his yellow jacket then marched to the door. On the back of Jenson's jacket, just below STT SECURITY, someone had written ASS in a thick black marker. Five seconds after he slammed the door, the room erupted with laughter.

"Who did it?" Evan asked.

"Better if no one knows," Vlad replied with an uncharacteristic smirk.

Evan changed into his uniform, took the radio and keys from the guard he was replacing, then hurried into the supervisor's office, which Jenson had left open. Since Evan had worked a few supervisory shifts, he knew where hard copies of incident reports were kept. Starting with the most recent, he worked backward, flipping through pages about bicycle and laptop thefts, altercations between students, dope in the dorms, propane smells, and first-aid accidents. Evan had to go back two months before he discovered that Stadler had filed a sexual harassment complaint against George Krenn. Whoa. Not what he'd expected, though Evan supposed he shouldn't be surprised. Nor was he surprised to see that Jenson had written the report on February fifteenth.

With serious incidents like this one, a copy was supposed to be sent to Okeyo for further investigation. He'd delegate the follow-up to one of two managers, then review their reports to determine what else should be done. All reports were locked in the managers' offices and a reference number noted on the original complaint. But this complaint had no number, and it should have had by now.

Evan looked at the calendar pinned to the bulletin board. He thought back to February and realized pretty quickly that neither of the managers would have been assigned Stadler's complaint. One of them had been on maternity leave since December. Jenson kept tabs of all supervisors and managers' time off schedules on the calendar. Evan flipped the pages back. The second manager had started vacation the day before Stadler filed the complaint. He'd also been away all this week.

Had Jenson kept the complaint from

Okeyo? How long did he think he would get away with it? Okeyo periodically checked these files to ensure that paperwork was properly completed.

"Hey, Evan," a co-worker called out. "Turn up your radio. Jenson wants you to monitor a couple of guys scoping out cars in the admin parking lot."

Evan put the binders away then glanced at the PC. He still wanted to know if the cameras had picked up any footage of Krenn before his death. Too bad it would have to wait.

Three hours passed before Evan found time to check out Veronica Stadler's schedule. Her partially open door would make lingering impossible. He'd have to steal a quick glance. If that didn't work, he'd come back once she was in class. Evan was still several feet away when he heard a cheerful female voice inside. Leaning against the wall, he listened to the one-sided conversation. Stadler had to be on the phone. He shuffled closer to the door.

"I'll be there by nine-thirty," she said, then paused. "No, I can't text you because the cops still have my phone...Of course I know it. Four, two, six, one."

Holy shit. That was the code for admin. Evan leaned against the wall. She had to be meeting Nigel Gardner. He was the only administrator who stayed late.

Stadler ended her conversation with a "See you soon," then hung up. Evan held his breath. From six feet away, he squinted to read the schedule. Stadler had taught last night. He turned and was about to leave when ferocious barking made him jump. The dog was halfway out the door and looking ready to attack.

"Adonis, down!" Stadler ordered. She poked her head outside. "Oh. It's you. I've seen you around."

Evan recalled exchanging brief nods while passing Stadler in hallways. "I saw the open door and thought I should check it out."

Adonis growled again. Apparently, he wasn't buying the explanation. Evan gaped at the dog's jowly face and enormous paws. The beast probably weighed as much as he did.

"Don't worry about Adonis," Stadler said. "He's a lamb. Well, a Great Dane, actually, but an old one." She sat down and crossed her arms beneath gigantic boobs that damn near blinded him in that neon yellow blouse. "You're the bike patroller, right?"

"Yes."

"No wonder you're so fit." Stadler looked him up and down. "What's your name?"

"Evan Dunstan."

Her face reminded Evan of the popovers his mother made with roast beef dinners. Puffy and golden brown, although not necessarily even all over. She'd either had trouble at the tanning salon or her skin was in rough shape.

"Were you, by any chance, the guard who found George Krenn last night?"

The edge in Stadler's voice made him wary. "I was, yeah."

"Bummer. For you, that is. As for Krenn..." She shrugged.

Since she'd raised the topic, Evan seized his chance. "May I ask you something?"

"That depends on the question."

"I was thumbing through reports recently and saw a harassment complaint from you against Mr. Krenn."

Stadler's puffy golden face started to pucker. "What about it?"

"No follow-up was referenced on the initial report." Evan cleared his throat. "I was wondering if anyone talked to you about the situation?"

As Stadler studied him, Evan tried not to stare at her boobs.

"I can see why this matters now," Stadler said. "But I'm curious as to why you're the one asking."

Evan scrambled for a reasonable explanation. "I came across it while I was looking for something else. The report caught my eye because it's irregular to have no follow-up reference number on a complaint that's two months old. I guess I'm just trying to figure out if protocol was followed or whether it was an oversight."

"I'm sure the police are wondering the same thing, given what I told them." Stadler's eyes glinted. "Are you certain that checking up on protocol is what you're after?"

Evan glanced at the dog who looked like he too expected an answer. At the moment, he was far more worried about Stadler than Adonis.

"I'm absolutely sure." Evan tried hard not to squirm as she looked him over again.

"Is this sudden diligence to protect your higher-ups or expose their missteps?"

"The latter," Evan replied. "If our site supervisor messed up, then it needs to be addressed."

"Is he the short guy with red hair?"

"That's him. Jenson Morlee's name is on the initial report."

"Thought so. Your site supervisor is a useless little shit."

"You won't get any argument from me," Evan replied. "Did George Krenn continue to harass you after you filed the complaint?"

Stadler scowled. "He was the one who told me that the complaint wasn't going anywhere. But at least Krenn backed down, more or less."

Jenson must have given Krenn a heads up. "Unbelievable."

"I can guess the other thing you're looking for, but are too scared to ask. So, let me assure you that I didn't kill Krenn." Stadler's eyes sparkled. "But I'm thrilled that he's gone."

"I don't think you're the only one."

"No doubt," she replied. "You should also know that going over your supervisor's little red head won't help your quest for the truth."

"Oh?"

"I also went to your director about the complaint and he did diddly squat, *which* I told the RCMP after they conveniently found my phone in the stream." Stadler studied Evan. "Funny thing. I know that I left the phone in my desk drawer and my office door locked while I taught last night. I also know that the instructor next door heard Adonis barking like mad while I was away because I got a nasty email from the jerk." She kept her gaze fixed on Evan. "Makes you wonder just how corrupt your bosses are, doesn't it?"

No way. From the day he started this job, all Evan had heard about was Okeyo's fairness and determination to see that things were done properly. He witnessed it himself many times. Okeyo Abasi was a complete professional who'd never say or do anything to make anyone question his actions.

"I don't think Mr. Abasi's like that."

Stadler snorted. "Just how well do you know the guy?"

Evan didn't know how to answer that. The truth was that Okeyo kept to himself. Rarely disclosed much about his personal life. All Evan knew was that he was a widower who was putting two of his three kids through university.

"Figure it out, Sherlock," Stadler added. "But you should know that George Krenn turned this campus into his own personal fiefdom and made lots of enemies along the way. There's a long list of suspects, kid." She turned away and started typing.

Chapter Seven

Evan's head was spinning. Why hadn't Okeyo followed up on Veronica Stadler's complaint, unless Krenn had been blackmailing him? But what could Okeyo have possibly done to become the sleazebag's victim? He'd have to be careful about what he said to anyone. *Think like a cop. Consider all possibilities.* As Evan replayed the highlights of his conversation with Stadler, he wondered if she'd been fully honest, especially about Okeyo. The cougar could have been messing with him. How the hell would he figure out truth from lies? Evan's phone rang.

"Learn anything new?" Sully asked.

He decided not to mention his chat with

Stadler. "No. Are you still in the plumbing building?"

"Hell, yeah. It took forever to finish my project, but I don't want trouble with Chourki, especially if he winds up with Krenn's job. Do you want to search this place with me now?"

"Like I thought, Jenson's been on my ass all night."

"Leads grow cold after the first forty-eight, dude. We can't wait."

Evan heard dispatch calling him. "Sully, I gotta go. Have a quick look, then call when you're ready to leave. If I get some time, I'll drop by."

"Gotcha, boss."

Evan spent the next half hour completing tasks until Sully called to say that Vlad had kicked him out of the building before he'd finished searching.

"We should go back in," Sully said.

"Can't. Classes are almost over and I've got to lock up parking kiosks."

"What if we sneak in after work?"

"Actually, I want to review all CCTV footage for last night."

"When's your next shift?" Sully asked.

"Tomorrow morning. Asshole put me on

the day shift."

"This could work. I have a class at nine. See ya, Five-O."

As classes ended, Evan was sent to escort several female students to their vehicles. Security's safe-walk program was rarely used, but Krenn's death had triggered a spike in requests.

At nine-thirty, Evan completed the last request, then hopped on his bike and rode to the admin building. He wasn't sure what he hoped to accomplish. Maybe he just needed to see Gardner and Stadler together, to gather his own proof. It seemed weird that Gardner, a married man with a prestigious job, would take this kind of risk for Veronica Stadler. Between the guards and the janitorial crew, people were bound to see them sooner or later. If Krenn knew, then Jenson probably did too. But how many others?

A couple of fourth-floor offices in the health sciences building looked directly into Gardner's office. Evan propped his bike against the HS building, then glanced up. The light in Gardner's office was on.

He swiped his card and was entering the alarm deactivation code when he heard,

"What the fuck are you doing, Dunstan?"

Shit! He hadn't heard Jenson pull up in that stupid hybrid. Why was Jenson here anyway? The lazy moron rarely ventured out of his office unless he was playing spy.

"I saw a light on the top floor in admin," Evan replied. "Thought I saw someone in Mr. Gardner's office."

"How about Mr. Gardner, numb-nuts?"

"I thought he went home earlier."

"Then don't just stand there. Check it out!" Jenson glared at him. "One other thing. Have you been screwing around with my black felt pen?"

Evan tried not to smile. "No. Why?"

"Cut the dumb act. I know everyone saw the jacket."

Evan coughed a little, then cleared his throat, but the grin popped out anyway. "I assumed it was your doing. You know, an acronym for Assistant Security Supervisor."

Jenson scowled. "You'll get yours, wiseass." He sped off.

Evan glanced up and saw Gardner at the window. Uh-oh. He must have heard Jenson. Evan took off on the bike. When he was clear of admin, he stopped and pulled out his notebook. Seeing as how covering one's ass was a huge part of the job, he jotted down a reference to seeing the light in Gardner's office, Jenson's request to check it out, and Gardner's appearance at the window.

The rest of Evan's shift flew by, thanks to the many tasks Jenson had him complete. This time, Evan didn't mind. The quicker the shift ended, the quicker he could look at the footage. Although hacking into it from home would be simple enough, he needed to know what the graveyard supervisor, Zach, had heard about Krenn's murder.

At the end of his shift, Evan was relieved to see Jenson take off in a hurry. The guy wasn't usually in a rush, but with Krenn dead, the jerk had no reason to hang around. At Evan's request, Zach described what little he knew about the previous night. He showed Evan two bookmarks to key footage that had already been burned onto a CD for the cops. Ordinarily, Zach was a rule follower who wouldn't let guards review footage, but Evan had done a couple of favours for him in the past.

"Okeyo had me review every camera on campus," Zach said, "to see who was on the premises. It took the entire shift to go through everything, but the only interesting stuff I found was by the stream. Cameras twenty-one and twenty-two have bookmarked segments. The first is ten minutes long, the second's a half hour."

"No one works those cameras better than you." Given that Corporal Renton hadn't asked to see Evan again, he figured he hadn't been spotted.

"Jenson wanted to review everything himself but Okeyo said no, which pissed Jenson off." Zach grinned. "It was cool."

"No doubt. So, what's in the interesting bits?"

"One individual in both bookmarks. The first looks like it could be Krenn." Zach paused. "You know people from the afternoon shift better than me. Maybe you can ID the other guy."

"I'll give it a shot."

As Zach left the room, Evan clicked on the first bookmark which began at 9:35 p.m. The camera slowly scanned the stream before stopping at the footbridge. There was no sign of anyone until 9:40, when someone in a dark tuque and clothing sauntered into the shot.

Although the individual had his back to the camera, Evan was convinced that the hefty build belonged to Krenn. He walked unsteadily along the stream's bank. Evan froze the image, then magnified it. The guy's coveralls were the type that plumbing instructors wore. The vodka bottle dangled from his hand. It was Krenn all right. Evan resumed the footage, but the camera soon moved in another direction. Damn. Why would dispatch do that? Hadn't it been obvious that the guy was off kilter? The footage ended.

The second bookmark showed a different angle of the stream. The footage also began at 9:35 p.m., however nothing happened until 9:55, when the camera panned back to reveal more of the stream's bank. Evan spotted a dark-clad figure walking away in the distance. His stride was steadier and quicker than Krenn's. Hurried. Again, Evan froze the image. This person wore black pants and a hoodie. Evan enlarged the image. This second individual was shorter than Krenn. Evan's cell phone rang.

"Hey, boss. Did you get a chance to look at the cameras?"

"I'm doing that now." Why did Sully need to know everything right away?

"See anything?"

"Not much."

As Evan stared at the dark figure, he realized that this person's build was similar to Sully's. When Sully wasn't in coveralls he sometimes wore black pants and a hoodie. Well, hell!

Chapter Eight

Bleary eyed, Evan trudged into the locker room at 6:45 a.m. Saturday morning. He despised early shifts, and this day was already off to a weird start. While he'd been making breakfast, Gran—who always rose early—came by to tell him that she'd spotted someone knocking on his door around nine the previous night.

"He was dressed in black from head to toe, Evvy," she'd said. "I couldn't even see his face."

She also said that he was taller and more muscular than Evan. A couple of buddies were built like that and often dropped by for a beer. Odd that none of them had texted him, though.

Evan put on the wide belt equipped with loops and pockets for flashlights, latex gloves, keys, and other equipment. A radio check showed that the battery was low. Not eager to go outside on this chilly morning, Evan took his time fetching fresh batteries and strapping on his helmet. Once the gloves were on, he headed outside, then regretted it instantly.

Corporal Renton was emerging from a dark sedan. What was he doing here so early? Torn between wanting to escape Renton's attention and wanting to know what he was up to, Evan hesitated. Based on the guy's grim expression, he either had a serious matter to discuss or he wasn't a morning person either.

For a panicky moment, Evan wondered if he was about to be charged with obstruction of justice for not reporting Krenn immediately, for allowing important clues to be washed away in the rain. The thought had been in back of his mind, causing a second night of restless sleep.

"Morning, Mr. Dunstan." Renton strolled toward him. "Have you seen or heard from Mr. Abasi since Thursday night?"

Not the question Evan had expected. "No." He'd assumed that Okeyo was in meetings all day yesterday to deal with the fall-out from Krenn's death.

"Would you, by any chance, have access to his office?"

Whoa. "No, but there's a key on the ring that shift supervisors share. Jenson and Okeyo are the only ones who have their own keys."

"Is Mr. Morlee here today?"

"Just the shift supervisor. I'll show you where she is."

Now that Evan thought about it, Okeyo's absence yesterday was kind of strange. He recalled Veronica Stadler's comment about Okeyo burying her complaint. Was it possible?

Evan found the supervisor, Sheila, in the small storage room where lost and found items were kept. Clipboard in hand, she appeared to be taking inventory. After Evan made the introductions, Renton lost no time asking about Okeyo.

"I haven't seen or heard from him lately," Sheila said.

"Is that normal?" Renton replied.

She hesitated. "Okeyo usually lets shift

supervisors know if he'll be in meetings or off campus. Supervisors pass the information on, but I haven't heard anything since Thursday night."

"I need to look in his office" Renton said.

Sheila gave Evan a pensive glance. "May I ask why?"

Renton didn't answer right away. "Basically, I'm just looking for a clue to his whereabouts. An appointment calendar or something."

"I can help with that. Okeyo keeps a paper calendar on his desk." She paused. "You aren't going to take anything away, are you? I mean, if you want to do a thorough search you'll need a court order, correct?"

"Correct. It's just a quick look at the calendar. You're welcome to stay and watch."

"All right." She turned to Evan. "You can go."

"Okay."

But Evan's gut told him that Renton was looking for more than an itinerary and that Stadler was right after all. Why would Okeyo set himself up for trouble like this?

He didn't seem the type to have legal or women problems, and certainly no addiction issues. Maybe the managers or his admin assistant knew how he spent his free time, but they weren't around to ask.

Evan stepped outside and hopped on the bike. He hadn't ridden far before a co-worker waved him over.

"Some chick was asking about you a few minutes ago."

"What'd she look like?"

"Hot. Long brown hair and green eyes. I think she's a student."

Cecelia. Awesome. "Where'd she go?"

She was going for a jog off campus. She asked when you started work and I said you were already here. She wants you to call her later."

"Okay, thanks."

"Watch out for Morlee," the guard said. "If he finds out that you're hooking up with a student you're toast."

His smirk suggested that Jenson would definitely find out. "What makes you think it's a hookup? What if has something to do with info about Krenn's murder?"

The smirk vanished. "You know something?"

"Someone sure as hell does." He rode away.

Evan was nearly across campus when his phone rang. He should have known it would be Sully.

"Class doesn't start for an hour," Sully said. "Let's search now."

"You're on campus already?"

"I want to get going."

Evan thought of the short dark figure he saw on the bookmarked footage. "We can't search yet. That cop Renton is back."

"What? Why?" Sully sounded panicky. "What does he want?"

"He's looking for Okeyo. But he could be here for other reasons. What if he decides to go through the plumbing building?"

"I need to disappear. Call me when he's gone."

Sully was looking more suspicious by the minute. There had to be a way to determine if it was guilt or just paranoia.

By the time, Evan finished his first patrol of the campus, Sully's class had started. Whether he was inside or not was another matter. As Evan rode past HQ, he saw that Renton's sedan was gone.

Had Renton found whatever he was

really looking for in Okeyo's office? He wouldn't be surprised if Jenson Freakin' Morlee had been badmouthing Okeyo to the police, enticing them to take a closer look at Okeyo's life. But Okeyo wasn't the type of man to run from a fight. Unless...Evan didn't want to think about it.

Over the next two hours, Evan had little time to come up with a plan to establish Sully's innocence. Dispatch kept sending him everywhere. Most of the calls were from instructors who'd left classroom keys at home and stupid students who kept tripping alarms to computer labs. Every lab had hours posted on their doors. How hard could it be to read a damn sign? Man, he needed a break. Evan pulled out his phone and called Cecelia.

"I was told that you're working the day shift," she said.

"Which means I have the evening off." He took a deep breath. "So, I was wondering if you'd like to go to a movie."

"Sure. That'd be great."

Evan's heart leapt. No hesitation. In fact, she sounded happy. "What would you like—" His radio crackled.

"Alpha Two," dispatch called.

"Someone's reported a bag of garbage floating in the stream. Can you check it out ASAP?"

Shades of Thursday night's horror flashed through his mind. "Cecelia, I have to go."

"I heard. Hope everything's okay. Call me."

"Definitely." Evan took a deep breath, then reached for his shoulder mic. "Ten-four, dispatch. Where in the stream?"

"Near the footbridge at engineering."

Evan paled. The same spot where he'd found Krenn. "Ten-four."

At least he was in daylight this time, and plenty of people were around. The football team had been heading toward the field for practice a few minutes ago. Lightning couldn't possibly strike twice.

The closer Evan got to the stream, the larger his anxiety grew. Sometime between last night and this morning, the police tape had vanished. Holding his breath, Evan rode up to the bank. He scanned the water and then gasped.

A black bulky object floated under the footbridge. Evan pedalled along the bank, past the bridge. His heart pounded as he left the bike and approached the water. The bag was about to appear. One of the football players spotted him and began jogging toward the stream.

"Everything okay?" the player asked.

"I'll know in a second."

"They found a teacher in here the other day."

Evan kept his gaze on the water. "I heard."

As the object floated nearer, the player said, "What the hell is that?"

Something round and light protruded from the bag.

"Not again!" Nausea roiled in Evan's stomach.

While more of the players came forward, Evan couldn't quite believe what he was seeing. An inflated pink balloon was attached to the top of the bag. Round eyes, bushy eyebrows, and a gaping mouth had been drawn on the balloon with a thick black marker. Inflated latex gloves protruded from each side of the bulky bag. Police tape was wound around the bag with a sign that said, HELP! I CAN'T SWIM!

"For shit's sake," Evan muttered, his face growing warm.

The team burst out laughing. The first player grinned as he looked at Evan. "You the guy who found the teacher?"

He sighed. "Yep."

"You been pranked bro'."

"Ya think?" Evan's already warm face grew hotter.

By this time a couple of guys were on their knees from laughing so hard. The coach tried to call them back to the field, but no one seemed to be listening.

Evan's radio crackled. The dispatcher snickered as he reported that they had the object on camera. "Think you can pull this one out of the water, Alpha Two?"

"I'll manage." So, which of his asshole colleagues had come up with the idea?

Evan grabbed the latex glove. The bag was so light that it took no effort to haul it onto the bank. As Evan dismantled the thing, the team reluctantly returned to practise, but not before one of them had snapped a few photos. Evan's phone rang.

"Is the cop still there?" Sully asked.

"No. I gather class is finished?"

"Yeah. Chourki left, but let me stay to keep looking for Krenn's hiding spots. I think I found something."

"What?"

"I remembered seeing Krenn move a cabinet out from a wall a few weeks back. He must have thought I'd gone home."

"Maybe he was just rearranging things."

"Come on, dude. George Krenn never did any physical labour unless he had to. I just finished dragging the cabinet away from the wall and found a loose cinder block. But I need your long spidery fingers to help me get it out."

If Sully was guilty, he wouldn't be asking for help, not with all those tools in the room.

"I'll meet you at the south entrance," Evan said.

He lifted his foot and popped the balloon head.

Chapter Nine

Evan propped his bike against the wall, then searched for the correct key among the fifteen on the ring. The trade buildings were actually warehouses purchased from a company that had relocated across the country. Given that trades didn't house as much hi-tech equipment as other buildings, STT had skimped on expensive alarm systems. Thankfully, CCTV cameras didn't cover this entrance.

Evan opened the door and stepped into a sparsely lit hallway. "You look kind of freaked out," he said to Sully.

"I keep hearing noises. Like somebody's moving something around." He glanced over his shoulder. "I heard that some of these buildings are haunted. Krenn's probably come back to make my life hell for all eternity."

Evan rolled his eyes. "Right. The ghosts of plumbers past."

Best not to admit that he'd heard about campus hauntings from day one. Sightings allegedly occurred after midnight, but Evan never worked that late and didn't believe the stories. Still, Sully had good reason to worry about not being alone. Assuming that he was innocent, then the killer could also be hunting for a blackmail list.

"Relax, Sully. It's probably mice."

"That's what they all say," he muttered. "Until evil jumps out and starts gnawing on your face."

"Have you been watching horror movies again?"

"Just a couple."

Switching on his flashlight, Evan followed Sully down the hallway. The heat was shut off and the concrete floor oozed a chilly dampness.

"I searched Chourki's office," Sully said, glancing at the closed door.

"How'd you get in?"

"Used a piece of gum to keep it from

latching properly. Crime shows aren't totally useless, dude. Anyway, all I found was a photocopy of a letter to the university prez describing Krenn's temper and drinking problem."

In the main room, Evan smelled soldered metal. Tables were covered with tools. Two rows of partitioned work stalls ran down the centre of the room.

"Over here." Sully headed to the west wall.

Evan studied four grimy horizontal windows on the upper half of the wall. Enough light came through to clearly see the cabinet that Sully had moved.

"Give me a hand," Sully said, ducking behind the cabinet.

Evan heard a scuffling sound further along the wall.

Sully jumped up. "Did you hear that?"

"Yeah."

"Someone's here!" Sully pushed past Evan and started to run until he smacked against a small table. Tools clanged onto the floor.

"Sully, stop. No one's here." Although the room was silent again, Evan didn't want to admit that he could be wrong. Truth was, he sensed that they were being watched. "Like I said, it's probably mice," he whispered. "Show me the loose cinder block."

"It's this one." Sully touched the third block from the bottom.

Evan wedged his fingertips into the narrow crack. The block barely moved. "I need a long flat tool to pry it out."

Sully retrieved a tool from the floor. "Try this."

Sully could have done this himself. Was he that afraid of being alone or did he want a witness to whatever he found? Evan removed the block, then plunked it on the floor. He shone the flashlight into the hole.

"Something's there." Reaching inside, he removed a zip-locked bag.

"That's it!" Sully exclaimed. "Krenn's blackmail list."

"Sshh." Evan glanced around the room.

"Open it," Sully urged.

Think like a cop. Evan removed latex gloves from the pouch on his belt. He'd barely got them on when he heard more scuffling.

Sully spun around. "There it is again!"

An enormous rat scurried across the

floor.

"Aggh!" Sully's arms flailed and he crashed into the table again, sending the rest of the tools to the floor.

"Jesus, Sully. Do you want the whole campus to know we're here? The rat's more afraid of you than you are of it."

"So you say." Sully's fearful eyes followed the rodent until it disappeared into the partitions.

Evan removed the sheets from the bag, then carefully unfolded them. "This is weird."

"What?" Sully moved closer.

"There's two pages. One is a screen shot of a cell phone for sale on eBay. The second is a typed list of other phones and electronic gadgets with prices and dates beside them. A gmail address is handwritten at the bottom." Evan showed the sheet to Sully. "Recognize it?"

Sully shook his head. "What's this about?"

Evan examined the list. Some of the descriptions sounded vaguely familiar, but from where?

Sully bent down and peered into the hole. "No blackmail list. Krenn must have another hiding spot."

"I'll check the mechanical room."

Evan grunted as he helped Sully maneuver the cinder block back into place. They pushed the cabinet against the wall then started to pick up the tools when the north door rattled. Evan froze.

"Bathroom!" Sully whispered, and took off.

Evan bolted after him, surprised that Sully was leading him into the women's room. They barely made it inside before his radio crackled.

"All units, code red," the dispatcher announced.

A fire alarm. They happened more often than Evan liked, and all had been false alarms. But protocol needed to be followed. Evan cracked open the door and heard a nearby voice say, "Ten-four." Evan peeked out and saw his co-worker leave the building.

"I have to go to the main fire panel and stay there until the fire department gives the all-clear," he told Sully.

"How long will that take?"

"Thirty minutes, give or take. Once I reset the panel, I'll come back if I have time." Evan stepped outside, then acknowledged the call.

"Timing's kind of amazing, don't ya think?" Sully said from the doorway.

Evan shrugged. "Contractors are on campus. They trip them all the time."

"If you unlock the mechanical room, I'll start searching."

"Not a good idea. If the guard comes back before I do then we're both in deep shit." Evan took another step outside, then stopped. "Where the hell is my bike? I left it propped next to the door. Shit! Someone took my freakin' bike!"

"Base to Alpha Two?" dispatch called.

"Go ahead," Evan replied.

"What's your twenty?"

"Plumbing building, but there's an issue." Evan quickly explained the situation.

"All units," dispatch announced. "Be on the look-out for Alpha Two's bicycle."

Evan grimaced at the "ten-fours" which were followed by chuckles and idiotic comments.

"You lead a glamorous life, dude," Sully remarked.

"Says the guy who's learning how to unclog toilets for a living." Evan began jogging toward the admin building.

Chapter Ten

Although his shift ended three hours ago, Evan still found it hard to unwind. Work had turned into an exasperating mess. Sully kept badgering him to return to the plumbing building, but there'd been reports to write and too many tasks on the crappy backup bicycle. Dispatch had spotted a scrawny guy riding off campus on Evan's bike, but then he'd disappeared.

With any luck, Evan would forget about this day once he was with Cecelia. He didn't look forward to going back on campus to pick her up, but at least the dorms were well away from Birch Stream and the plumbing building.

The microwave beeped. Evan removed

the fried chicken TV dinner onto the counter. While it cooled, he returned to the list of electronics he and Sully had found. Evan had discovered that most of the items had been sold by the owner of the mysterious gmail account. The other two columns represented the date of purchase and amount paid. The longer Evan studied the list, the more something wriggled in the back of his brain. A tiny bit of recognition. Wait...hadn't he brought a couple of these items to the lost and found at HQ?

Every time someone turned an item in, dispatchers recorded the info on an Excel worksheet. If the property wasn't claimed after two months, the cheap stuff went to recycling or trash bins. Electronics were given to Okeyo or Jenson for proper recycling. Shit. Was this Jenson's little side business? Too bad that the eBay info only showed that the seller was based in Canada and had been in business for three months.

Evan wished he had time for more research, but hot dates required preparation. He started in on the chicken until someone knocked on the door. It could be family. On the other hand, Gran had said that someone came looking for him last night. Buddies often dropped by on Saturdays to mooch food and beer. Evan opened the door and inhaled sharply.

"Hello, Evan," Okeyo said. "May I come in?"

"Uh." Evan cleared his throat. "Sure."

When Okeyo stepped inside, it felt as if the air had just been sucked out of the room. His massive body filled Evan's space.

"I realize that coming here is odd," Okeyo said. "But I needed to talk to you urgently and privately."

Part of Evan wanted to ask why. Another part wasn't sure he wanted to know. The tension emanating from Okeyo made Evan nervous. He didn't know what to say to the man, so he blurted, "Corporal Renton was looking for you this morning."

"I'm sure he was." Okeyo's blank expression didn't change. "But I needed some downtime to think things through." He zeroed in on Evan's computer. "Did you and Mr. Sinh La find anything interesting in the plumbing building this afternoon?"

Evan's heartbeat quickened. "You were there?"

"For a short while."

So, he *had* been watched. Evan didn't

know whether to feel relieved or more worried.

"I saw the kid who stole your bike," Okeyo added. "My car was nearby, so I tailed him to a house fifteen minutes from here. I got the address and called police."

"Thanks. I appreciate it."

Okeyo picked up the eBay sheets and looked them over.

"I didn't make that list," Evan blurted. "That's what we found in the wall."

Okeyo folded the papers. "What, exactly, do you know about George Krenn's extra-curricular activities?"

"Almost nothing. But someone told me that he ran STT like his own personal fiefdom." Evan paused. "And that he kept a list of people he was blackmailing. Since all we found were those sheets, I'm not sure that's true."

"It is."

Evan's eyebrows rose. He waited, but Okeyo didn't elaborate. Instead, his dark, unblinking eyes simply stared at him. Sully was right. There had to be another hiding spot.

"Why did you two take it upon yourselves to look?" Okeyo asked.

"To clear our names. Mr. Chourki said that we're at the top of Corporal Renton's suspect list." Evan met Okeyo's gaze. "Any idea why?"

Okeyo shook his head. "Whatever Renton might have heard didn't come from me. I don't believe for one minute that you had anything to do with Krenn's death."

Evan noticed that he didn't mention Sully.

"Who told you that Krenn ran a personal fiefdom?" Okeyo asked.

Right now, keeping things from his boss didn't seem like a good idea. "Veronica Stadler."

Okeyo broke eye contact and sighed. "She's correct."

"Oh." Evan didn't know what else to say.

"I can't speak for Ms. Stadler," Okeyo added. "But I didn't kill Krenn."

"I never thought you did."

"You must have concluded by now that I was one of his victims." Okeyo gazed at the sheets he still held.

Evan's eyebrows rose. "I didn't, actually."

"This gmail account is mine."

Not what he wanted to hear. "I thought it might have been Jenson's. Given what Ms. Stadler said about no one following up on her harassment complaint, I figured that he and Krenn were working together."

"They were. But that's only part of the picture," Okeyo replied. "I'm ashamed to admit that Veronica Stadler called me, asking why no one had done anything about her complaint. I didn't even know it existed until I approached Jenson. The next day, Krenn dropped by my office and showed me these sheets. That's when I understood the size of the net I was caught in." He glanced at the sofa. "Do you mind if I sit down?"

"Sure."

Okeyo plunked down heavily, then rested his elbows on his thighs. "That bastard Jenson put me under Krenn's control."

"How?"

"Jenson caught me putting lost and found items into my backpack. I tried to convince him that they'd be taken to a recycling depot, but it turns out the little shit also has an eBay account. I don't know how long Jenson had been taking items before me, but he soon realized that his stash was mysteriously depleting."

"But you kept selling the stuff?"

"Had to. Jenson told Krenn about my side business and rather than shut me down, Krenn encouraged me to keep selling, for fifty percent of the profit. That way, he kept me under control." Okeyo lowered his head. "My youngest will be joining his brother and sister at university next year. It's impossible to pay all that tuition on one income. Selling unclaimed items seemed harmless enough."

Except that it was against campus policy. Guards weren't even supposed to remove pop bottles from recycling bins to sell, never mind electronics.

"I don't know if it's a coincidence or not, but this morning Sheila was taking inventory of lost and found," Evan said.

"Saturday supervisors do it every six weeks, but I'm sure Jenson's changed the spreadsheet to make it appear that everything's accounted for." Okeyo paused. "I have a feeling he wants to take over Krenn's operation."

"Not good."

"He'll have to be stopped." Okeyo crumpled the sheets in his huge hands.

"That's why I've come here. We need to find evidence that Jenson was helping Krenn find blackmail candidates."

"Without some sort of paper trail that will be hard."

"Not necessarily," Okeyo replied. "I don't think Krenn manipulated or conspired with anyone unless he had leverage, and I think it's highly likely that he had something on Jenson."

"But they got along well."

Okeyo nodded. "I think Jenson opted to join him rather than fight him."

"Figures," Evan mumbled. "Do you know who else Krenn was blackmailing?"

Okeyo rubbed his face. He seemed to age before Evan's eyes. "Nigel Gardner. I found out when he showed me a blackmail note and demanded that I do something about Krenn."

"Which you couldn't, and which victimized Veronica Stadler a second time."

Okeyo's brow furrowed. "You know about those two?"

"Discovered their affair yesterday."

Okeyo nodded. "I regret that I couldn't help Gardner, but the stakes were too high. Now that Krenn's dead, I've had to rethink some things."

The living room wall began to rise.

"Oh, no." Evan spotted his grandmother's chicken legs and those of her friends. Soon, three ancient faces were gawking at Okeyo.

"Goodness," Gran said, holding a plate containing a slice of chocolate cake. "If I knew you had company, Evvy, I would have brought another slice. A much larger one."

"This is my boss, Okeyo Abasi," Evan said, turning to Okeyo. "And this is my grandmother and her friends, Flo and Agnes."

"A pleasure," Okeyo said. As he stood, the women gasped.

"You're a big one, aren't you," Flo murmured with obvious admiration.

"Spectacular," Agnes added, adjusting her bifocals.

Evan cringed.

"Were you here last night, by any chance?" Gran asked Okeyo. "I saw a big man like you outside Evan's door."

"Yes, but he wasn't home so I thought I'd try again."

"My grandson's not in trouble, is he?" Gran said to Okeyo. "Evvy's a good boy and a hard worker. Always does his chores."

Forcing a smile, Evan crossed his arms.

"He's just helping me out with something." Okeyo turned to Evan. "Isn't that right, son?"

"Yes." Although he still wasn't sure what Okeyo wanted from him.

"We've been celebrating Flo's birthday. She's eighty-five today and that definitely deserves cake. Would you like us to get you a piece, Mr. Abasi?"

"Thank you, but I have to leave in a minute."

"We want a game of cribbage before Flo nods off, so I'll just leave this on the table."

As the door lowered, Evan heard Agnes say, "Holy moly. I nearly wet my underpants."

Evan could barely look Okeyo in the eye. "Sorry about that."

"No problem." The amusement on Okeyo's face quickly faded. "Does Mr. Sinh La know about my eBay business?"

"He saw the sheets but doesn't know who the account belongs to."

"Good. Let's keep it that way."

"All right." Sully wouldn't be happy, but this was not the time to make an enemy of his boss.

"I'll tell Corporal Renton about it," Okeyo added. "But no else on campus is to know, understand?"

"Absolutely."

"And I'm shutting down the account. It's not worth the hassle or the self-loathing. I just hope that Renton won't say anything to the academic bigwigs." Okeyo paused. "You should also know that I'll help look for the blackmail list."

"That'd be great. Do you think the list will be long?"

"Long enough." Okeyo paused. "Those people were under Krenn's control because of secrets that needed to stay that way. God knows what they've done, or what they'll do to get incriminating information back."

Evan thought of Sully. "A scary prospect."

"That's why it's good that Mr. Sinh La is helping. Neither of you should search alone."

"Then you don't think Sully did it?" Evan blurted, regretting the question instantly. Okeyo's expression was both confused and suspicious.

"Do you?" he asked.

Evan cleared his throat. "The man walking away on the footage for camera twenty-two has Sully's build, and he seems almost too eager to find that list."

"I'll keep that in mind," Okeyo replied. "For whatever it's worth, though, my gut says he's not the killer."

"Glad to hear it." Relief washed over Evan. Despite what he learned tonight, he trusted Okeyo's instincts. Lapses in judgement made him human, not perfect.

Okeyo headed for the door. "Are you working tomorrow?"

"Tuesday," he replied. "I was going to check the mechanical room next. It's one of the few places Krenn probably had exclusive access to in that building."

"Not necessarily." Okeyo gripped the door handle. "He had a master key."

"Yeah, I figured. But how did you...Oh."

"It's what shames me most." Okeyo opened the door. "I'll call if I find anything, and please let me know if you discover that list. You have my personal cell number, correct?"

"Yes."

"One more thing. Watch out for Jenson. That deceitful, backstabbing bastard would like nothing more than to see you in jail."

The feeling was mutual, Evan thought.

Chapter Eleven

Evan grinned as he drove out of the dorm's parking lot. The date had gone well and he'd been smart enough not to push his luck. One goodnight kiss and that was it. But it had been an awesome kiss. They'd already made dinner plans for next weekend.

Evan cruised down the quiet industrial road next to the trades buildings on the west side of campus. He hadn't intended to go this way, yet here he was, his thoughts drifting to Okeyo's visit earlier. The sight of a familiar beat-up Corolla made Evan hit the brakes. What the hell was Sully doing here after midnight? Evan scanned what he could see of the campus. If Sully was in the plumbing building, had he snuck in while the guard was on a walk-through or had someone let him in? Maybe Okeyo was with him. Maybe he wasn't.

Evan pulled up behind the Corolla. Interesting that Sully had parked here. Campus cameras didn't reach this part of the street. Evan turned off the engine, then grabbed the black tuque and hoodie he kept in the back seat. He removed his jacket and pulled the hoodie on. The wind had picked up and it started to rain, giving him a reason to keep his head down and avoid recognition on camera.

As expected, no lights were on in the plumbing building. If Sully was inside, he had probably used the south entrance. Evan crept up to the door and tried the handle. Unlocked. No surprise there. Sully wasn't great with details. Evan peeked inside. He couldn't hear anything. Tiptoeing down the hallway, he shivered. The building was even colder and bleaker than it was in daylight. As Evan passed the women's washroom he heard a scratching sound inside. Evan edged closer to the door then cracked it open. A beam of light came from beneath the sink.

Evan stepped inside. "Why are you digging a hole in the floor?"

Sully looked up and smacked his head on the sink. "Ow!" He fell on his ass. "What are you doing here?"

"I was out with Cecelia. Dropped her off at the dorm, then saw your car as I was leaving." Evan noticed the grungy tile beside the hole. "How'd you get in the building?"

"Vlad let me in."

Evan remembered that he was working the graveyard shift.

"Vlad usually doesn't do anyone favours. How'd you manage it?"

"I, uh..." Sully lowered his head.

"It's a simple question."

"All right, look," Sully blurted. "He told me to find the list tonight or I'll be expelled on Monday."

"Vlad said that?"

"Not him."

"Who then?" Evan waited, but Sully didn't answer. "Come on, buddy. Talk to me."

"The CFO, Gardner." Sully looked up. "He told Vlad to let me in. Said he'd lost something important and needed me to look for it right away."

"Why would Gardner ask you to find the

list? Why not do it himself?"

"Guess he didn't want to take the time. Besides, he's used to having people do things for him," Sully muttered. "Gardner said that Krenn wanted me out of STT permanently, but Gardner refused."

"I'm surprised he stood up to Krenn."

"I think it was more a matter of stalling. Gardner knew that Krenn was a racist shithead, and that it would be a PR nightmare if I publically accused the STT of keeping guys like Krenn on the payroll."

"So, you're doing this for Gardner because you feel you owe him?"

Anguish crossed Sully's face. "Because he said he really would expel me if I didn't find that blackmail list tonight. He also wants some incriminating photos of him and a woman, who I'm guessing is Veronica Stadler."

"Terrific. Is Gardner on campus right now?"

"He was earlier. Don't know if he still is. I'm supposed to phone him when I find the stuff. He gave me his cell number." Sweat broke out on Sully's brow. "What if they both killed him?"

"Then we'd better stay out of their way."

Evan looked at the hole in the floor. "What made you search in here?"

"Process of elimination. I checked every cinder block in this place, then remembered seeing Krenn come in here once. He probably thought I'd gone." Sully paused. "I searched the walls but didn't find anything. When I was washing my hands I stepped on a loose tile." A gust of wind rattled the window. Sully jumped to his feet. "This place is even creepier at night."

"Did you find anything in the hole?"

"I was just about to find out."

Sully ducked under the sink, reached in and pulled out a clear plastic bag. Evan saw photos right away, along with a folded sheet of paper. He snatched the bag from Sully.

"Hey! I gotta take those to Gardner."

"Let's see what they are first."

"No! If he thinks I've seen them, I'm done!"

"He might expel you anyway, Sully. Shouldn't you keep a couple as leverage to make sure that doesn't happen?" Evan didn't want to resort to Krenn's tactics, but there was a big different between exploitation and protecting oneself from further abuse.

"If Gardner's the killer, he won't think

twice about stealing the photos back then getting rid of me," Sully said.

"Which is reason enough to give these to the cops right away. And don't worry about being expelled. Okeyo will stand up for you. He knows what's going on with Gardner."

"How do you know?"

Evan had no intention of spilling Okeyo's secret. "I can't go into that now. We have to get to HQ." As Evan stepped out of the bathroom he heard a noise from the main room.

"What's that?" Sully whispered behind him.

"I don't want to find out." He hurried down the short hallway.

Evan was pushing the door when someone yelled, "Stop!"

He looked over his shoulder to find Gardner pointing a gun straight at them.

Chapter Twelve

"Give me the photos, Sully," Gardner ordered.

"Evan has them!"

Evan bolted outside, Sully close on his heels.

The gun fired.

"Sully!" Evan called out. "You okay?"

"Yeah. He missed, but I'm outta here!" Sully veered off the path and darted between two buildings.

Evan raced toward a cluster of trees and bushes, praying that Gardner would have a tough time getting a clear shot. The blood pounded in his ears. He couldn't hear footsteps, just the rain falling on leaves.

Another shot rang out. Close! Too damn

close! Evan kept moving, wishing he could glance over his shoulder, but it was too risky. Every second counted. Sweeping raindrops from his eyes, he squinted into the darkness.

"Evan!" Gardner shouted. "I just want the photos! Don't make me hurt you!"

Although his voice sounded more distant, Evan ran harder. He turned the corner, scanning the grounds as he ran. HQ was at the other end of the main road that cut through the trades area. Right now, it felt far away. It would be faster to take the road, but it left him out in the open. Better to stay on the footpaths behind and between buildings, but would he make it in time? Gardner probably knew this campus as well as he did. He had to realize Evan's destination.

Evan slipped on a patch of mud and landed hard on one knee. Scrambling to his feet, he looked behind him, but didn't see Gardner. He pulled his phone from his pocket and dialed 911. As he ran, he explained what was happening.

"I'm almost at the security office." He gasped for breath. "It's at the southeast corner." As Evan left the footpath and cut across a patch of grass, the 911 call-taker asked if the gunman was alone. "I only saw him, but I don't know."

What if Veronica Stadler was here too? The wind picked up. To his right, Evan saw movement. Possibly a tree branch. More movement. A person. Oh, shit.

"Stay right there, Evan!" Gardner yelled, pointing the gun at him. "I just want the bag."

Even stopped and tried to breathe.

"I didn't kill Krenn," Gardner said. "Despite what it looks like, I don't want violence. I just want the photos. My wife and kids don't deserve a scandal."

The normally calm and cool CFO had never looked so agitated or dishevelled. His light brown hair stood straight up in places and he needed a shave.

"The cops are coming." As Evan gulped down air, he realized that he'd just cut off the 911 call. Damn.

"Good. Let them. Krenn's killer could be nearby," Gardner replied. "I was outside that night. Saw someone by the footbridge. Someone short and slim. That person killed him."

It was true that Gardner was too tall to

have been the individual Evan saw on the footage. And he'd described the suspect correctly, unless he'd seen the footage.

"Why didn't you say anything?"

"Because the police would want to know what I was doing near engineering."

"Why were you there?"

Gardner paused, as if deciding whether to answer. "Krenn wanted money from Veronica. She didn't have enough cash, so she called me. I was going to confront the son-of-a-bitch, record his demands." Gardner glanced around. "I stayed by the stream because it seemed unlikely that anyone would be there at that time of night. I saw Krenn in the water. Seconds later, you came along, so I took off back to the admin building."

"And you called security, pretending to have forgotten the code to give yourself an alibi."

"Yes."

"Then why the gun?" Evan asked, wiping rain from his eyes.

"To protect myself from the killer. Like I said, he's probably here, looking for whatever will incriminate him. We should be working together, Evan. Don't you see that?"

What Evan saw was a man accustomed to getting his way. But Gardner was right. Judging from the way his hand was shaking, he wasn't used to violence. His gut told him that the man truly didn't want to hurt anybody. He just wanted his life to return to normal.

"Evan?" Vlad called out from behind. "Is that you?"

Evan looked over his shoulder. "Yes. Cops are en route."

Vlad stepped closer and spotted Gardner. The gun didn't make him flinch. "What trouble is this?"

"No trouble," Gardner replied. "Just a conversation."

Vlad grunted, then called a code green on the radio.

"No!" Evan said. "If all the guards come to assist, then somebody could get shot."

Vlad looked unimpressed. "If this is simple conversation, why does CFO need gun?" He turned to Gardner. "Why not put it down?"

"I'm working on it," Evan murmured. "You should step out of range, in case I fail."

That Vlad stayed put didn't surprise Evan. The man had taken on more than his share of drunken students, thieves, and irate staff. A shaky accountant with a gun wouldn't send him running.

"Guards will be joining me in less than a minute," Evan said to Gardner. "A code green means that the dispatchers are patching into my radio and pointing cameras on us right now. Do you really want to be recorded shooting people?"

Gardner's hand shook so badly that he dropped the gun in a puddle. He gaped at the weapon as if he could hardly believe he'd done that. Gardner started to bend down.

"Don't!" Evan shouted.

Gardner froze. His dazed, fearful expression turned to panic and he took off.

Vlad shook his head. "Coward."

"He's just in over his head. Good thing he realized it or this could have ended badly," Evan replied. "Still, we should go in case Gardner remembers how badly he wants this bag."

"I'll get weapon." Vlad reached down to pick it up.

"Use gloves," Evan said. "You don't want your fingerprints on it."

"Smart boy." Vlad pulled out the latex gloves. Soon, the pair were hurrying toward HQ. The wind chilled Evan's face, forcing him to squint. His heart slammed against his chest as he wondered if Sully was okay.

"Did CFO kill Krenn?" Vlad asked.

"I doubt it."

Evan reached security's main entrance and was about to pull the door open when Cecelia appeared around the corner. She peered at him from under her umbrella. "Evan?"

"Cecelia! What are you doing here?"

"Couldn't sleep, so I went for a walk. Then I saw a guard running this way. He looked pretty worried." She glanced at Vlad before turning back to Evan. "Why are you still on campus? Has something happened?"

"Kind of."

Cecelia watched two more guards approach. "Does it have something to do with the plastic bag you're holding?"

"Yeah."

"What's in it?"

"Evidence to do with Krenn's murder."

Her eyes widened. "What kind of evidence?"

"Photos of people he was blackmailing

and possibly a list of victims." His co-workers looked at one another, but said nothing.

"Are you sure?" Cecelia asked. "Have you seen the pictures?"

"Haven't had time to look."

"Don't you think you should? What if you're wrong?"

"She's right, Evan." Jenson Freakin' Morlee appeared from the other end of the building. "Don't you think we should see what's in there before you look like a total moron?"

"What is shithead doing here?" Vlad muttered.

"Good question." Evan kept his gaze fixed on Jenson. Unlike Gardner, Jenson didn't look nervous. Every miserable strand of hair was in place, his red beard as neatly trimmed as ever. "Why are you here this late on a Saturday night?"

"I don't answer to you, dipshit. You answer to me."

"Not this time. What's your interest in this bag?"

"I don't have to tell you squat."

As Jenson stepped closer, Evan sensed the loathing. But something else.

Determination. Fury. This guy wouldn't recoil from violence. Evan studied the enemy's short slim stature, the way his hands curled into fists, and then he knew who'd killed Krenn.

"You three need to get back to work!" Jenson pointed at Vlad plus the other two guards.

"What's happening, Evan?" The graveyard supervisor, Zach, stepped out of the building.

Evan glanced over his shoulder. He spotted the guards' pensive faces. As Zach stepped forward, Evan said, "I found evidence that might tell us who murdered George Krenn, which is why Nigel Gardner pulled a gun on me and probably why Jenson's here. Isn't that right, Jenson?"

"Screw you." Jenson looked at the bag then removed a sharp-looking knife from his pocket. "You all report to me. You do what I tell you to, and I want that bag!"

"Evan?" Cecelia said, looking scared.

"Go inside," he said. "The cops have already been called." Evan glanced at his colleagues. "Could a couple of you make sure she's safe?"

The two guards escorted Cecelia toward

the door.

"I want that bag, damn it!" Jenson yelled.

"You get nothing!" Vlad moved closer to Evan's right.

"I found the photos and am handing them in," Evan said.

"You two are fired. Not get the hell out of here or I'll have you charged with trespassing."

"We'll see what Okeyo says about that," Zach replied, and took up position on Evan's left side.

"Okeyo." Jenson spat on the ground. "He's done."

"He's not," Evan replied. "Far from it."

Uncertainty flickered across Jenson's face. Raindrops fell from his red beard. He swiped the drops from his eyes. "You don't know anything, numb-nuts."

"Wanna bet your paycheque?"

Uncertainty transformed to a blank stare, followed by worry, and then more anger. "You're full of it, Dunstan."

"I hear sirens," a guard said from behind. "I think they're somewhere on campus."

"Get dispatch to find them on camera,

then bring them here," Zach ordered.

"You can't stop me!" Jenson's wild gaze darted from one to the other. "I own this place!"

"Bullshit, you stupid jerk!" Evan shot back.

"Useless shithead," Vlad muttered.

"All right," Zach cautioned. "Let's everyone calm down." He turned to Evan. "Maybe you should give me the bag and I'll lock it up."

"No. I got this," Evan replied. "The cops'll be here any sec—"

Jenson lunged for Evan, but Evan's reflexes were too fast. He leapt back. Jenson slashed the air, nearly slicing Vlad's arm in the process.

"You got trouble now!" He started for Jenson who raised the knife.

"Stay back!" Jenson yelled. "I mean it!"

Vlad didn't stay back. He stepped closer. He removed Gardner's gun from his pocket, then pointed it straight at Jenson. Exclamations of "shit" and "whoa" came from the guards behind them.

Evan was grateful that the big guy had kept the gloves on.

"Fuck!" Jenson jumped back.

"Vlad, no," Evan said. "You need your job, right?"

Vlad kept his focus on Jenson. "Maybe it's more important to rid world of big parasite."

"No, man. Better to let him rot in jail and think about what he's done."

"You're dead, Dunstan!" Jenson stepped backward and stumbled over a rock.

He tried to regain his footing, but Vlad was on him instantly, kicking Jenson in the shin with his size thirteen steel-toed boot.

"Ow! You bastard!" Jenson crumpled to the ground. The knife bounced out of his hand.

"You're right," Vlad said to Evan. "Pain is better than death for this animal."

While Jenson moaned, Zach snatched the knife away. "I'll take the gun too, Vlad. Better that the cops don't find it on you."

As Vlad handed him the weapon, Jenson started to get up but Vlad shoved him back down. "Stay, doggie!"

"Put the cuffs on him," Zach ordered.

"Don't you dare!" Jenson screamed.

As Jenson tried to get up again, Evan jumped in to help. He and Vlad soon had the site supervisor on his stomach and with his arms secured behind his back.

"Think that'll stop me?" Jenson thrashed and kicked out, nearly smacking Evan's ankle.

"We need to restrain his legs," Zach said.

"Get duct tape," Vlad said, glowering at the cursing Jenson. "Mouth needs shutting too."

Jenson struggled to get to his knees but Vlad had him on the ground again. This time he sat on him.

"Get off me!" Jenson yelled. "I'll sue for assault."

"I sue you for being moron," Vlad grumbled.

Cecelia ran up to Evan and covered his head with her umbrella. "Are you okay?"

"Yeah. But you should stay back. The guy's completely lost it," he replied, watching Jenson squirm and kick.

Sully reappeared. "Hey, boss."

"Where've you been?" Evan asked.

"I saw Gardner running, so I followed long enough to see him headin' north on Elmwood Street."

"Cops are almost here. Let them know." Although why they hadn't arrived yet baffled him. It seemed like ages since he'd called 911.

Zach reappeared, trailed by two guards. "Couldn't find the duct tape, but this'll do." Smiling, he handed Evan the long strip of police tape. "Found it sitting on top of a garbage bag."

"And I'm sure you saw the footage."

Zach laughed. His radio crackled. A guard was reporting that the cops were down by the dorms at the opposite corner of campus. Zach told him to bring them here.

"That's it?" Evan asked. "One patrol car for a gunman on campus?"

"Guess they're having a busy Saturday night," Zach replied. "Let me help you wrap this asshole's ankles."

It took some quick dodging and even quicker grabbing before each of them had a firm grip on Jenson's thrashing legs. While Vlad kept him pinned on the ground, Evan and Zach wrapped the tape around his ankles. Once he was immobile, Vlad got up but kept one boot on Jenson's back.

Sully and Cecelia moved closer.

"Way cooler than duct tape," Sully said. "Seeing as how the guy's a walking crime spree."

Zach turned to the guards who were still standing around, gaping. "Back to patrols, guys." His radio crackled again. Dispatch needed him to take a phone call inside.

As everyone dispersed, Evan opened the plastic bag. Cecelia held the umbrella over them and gently nudged against his arm. Sully stood on his other side.

"Don't you dare, you son-of-a-bitch!" Jenson's eyes bulged as he lifted his head.

"Why?" Evan asked. "What are you afraid of?"

Evan thumbed through a dozen photos. One was of Vlad helping himself to Krenn's whiskey. "You should have this." He handed it to Vlad.

Vlad stared at the photo. "Thanks." He slipped it in his pocket.

"That's tampering with evidence," Jenson said. "I'll make sure the cops know."

"You tried to kill me," Evan said. "If you don't want me pressing charges, then shut the fuck up!"

Another photo revealed a naked Gardner and Veronica Stadler on his desk.

"Oh, god," Cecelia murmured.

"Which one of the pervs took it?" Sully mumbled. "Krenn or his sidekick?"

Evan quickly moved the photo to the bottom of the stack, then stared at the next shot. "Your answer's right here."

Sully squinted and took a closer look. "Isn't that Jenson peeking through a hole in the wall between two sinks and mirrors?"

"Can I see that?" Cecelia asked. Without waiting for a response, she took the photo from Evan. The longer she examined the snapshot, the deeper her frown. "I knew it!" she said. "This was taken inside the men's bathroom in our dorm. The women's bathroom shares the same wall. It's even the same damn colour."

"So, your site supervisor's a creep in every sense of the word." Sully stared at Jenson. "Pathetic, dude."

Vlad glared at Jenson and shifted his boot.

"Ow!" Jenson winced. "Stop!"

"We found the hole a while ago and figured that someone was watching us," Cecelia said. "By process of elimination, we thought the freak might be a guard, and we were right."

"George told me to take pictures!" Jenson yelled. "And you only went out with Dunstan because you thought he had inside information."

"Our first date was tonight." Cecelia scowled at Jenson. "How did you know about it?"

Jenson's smile was almost evil. "Not much gets by me."

"Especially if you're still spying on us," Cecelia shot back. "You were in the dorm tonight, weren't you, you bastard! Still peeping even after your buddy's dead. Check his phone, Evan."

Evan hesitated. Had she only gone out with him to gain information?

"Listen to me." Cecelia gripped his arm. "I knew you weren't the culprit. You're far too decent a guy. But I did hope that you'd help me figure out who was. Now that we know the truth, I still want to see you, if that's okay."

"It is." In fact, it was awesome. "But the cops are here." He nodded toward the strobing lights. "They should take his phone."

The RCMP cruiser slowly drew nearer. Clearly, the cops saw no urgency to the situation. Maybe they'd already heard that things were under control.

"Sully, you should tell the cops about

Gardner," Evan said.

"Ten-four, boss." He wandered toward the cruiser.

"Can you check to see if there are more bathroom shots in that bundle?" Cecelia whispered. "If there are, I want them pulled. It's a total invasion of privacy."

"I can't pull all of them," he whispered back. "The cops need evidence to press charges."

"Could you take any of me out?" she asked. "I just couldn't stand the idea of them being gawked at by cops or a jury. And what if one was leaked to the press?"

Evan glanced at Vlad. He'd gotten his photo back, so why shouldn't the woman of his dreams? Evan thumbed through eight shots, fully aware that Cecelia was leaning against him, her eyes fixed on the photos of partially nude women. Evan thought he recognized a couple of faces.

"There's none of you in here."

"Yeah, but three of my friends are," she answered. "Do you think Krenn would have blackmailed them too?"

"Eventually, maybe. Students don't have money, but once they got going in their careers, he might have tried to cash in."

"A long-term investment," she mumbled. "Then why is a photo of Jenson with this stack?"

"I think it was Krenn's means of keeping the bastard under control. Make sure he did whatever Krenn told him to." Like bury harassment complaints. Evan turned and glared at Jenson. "Krenn caught you in the act, but allowed you to keep your perverse little hobby if you did him favours and he got print copies of the photos, right?"

"He made me take pictures. It was all Krenn's doing," Jenson replied. "If I didn't cooperate he'd destroy me."

Evan didn't buy it. The pair were too friendly, always laughing and joking. Sure, Krenn had leverage, but Jenson embraced the game because Krenn let him keep a percentage of the cash from eBay sales, maybe even gave him a small cut of the extortion money.

Evan glanced at the half dozen names on the blackmail list. With the exception of Okeyo, each individual had an accompanying photo. Not all of the photos were sexual in nature, but in some way they must have compromised the victim's reputation. Among the names was a human resources executive, an IT technician, and the head of the maintenance department.

Two burly officers stepped out of the cruiser. Zach and Sully went up to them.

"You killed Krenn, didn't you?" Evan said to Jenson. "Your height and body type match a witness account, not to mention what we saw on the CCTV footage. You were at the stream, Jenson."

"No!" Jenson yelled. "The cops found Veronica Stadler's phone in the water. She's the guilty one!"

"Now I get it," Evan said. "You went to engineering to steal her phone. Easy to do since HQ's not far from here, and no one would be around at that time of night to see what you were up to."

"I was only in the area to help the newbie lock up. He was behind schedule."

The officers approached Evan, trailed by Zach and Sully.

"You did your best to implicate Stadler and anyone else who had problems with Krenn," Evan went on. "Hoping that something would stick."

"That's a lie!"

"The guy on the ground killed George Krenn," Sully said to the constables.

"Liar!"

"He also slashed at Evan with a knife," Cecelia added.

"They're making up stories!" Jenson's shouts had become a plea.

The cops stared at him without expression.

"We'll take those weapons now," one of them said to Zach.

"Sure. They're inside."

A second police cruiser showed up. After a quick consultation, one cop went inside HQ while the other approached Jenson.

"You're making a big mistake," Jenson yelled at them. "I'll sue for false arrest!"

"Why'd you do it, Jenson?" Evan blurted. "Why kill the only friend you had on campus?"

"He wasn't my friend! I was his slave. He wanted me to break into offices and rip off anything of value. I told him it was too risky and we argued, but Krenn wouldn't back down. The next day I brought him a vodka bottle, told him it was a peace offering."

"One spiked with some drug," Evan said.

"He said he'd be picking up cash from Stadler and celebrating with my vodka. I watched on camera. When he got near engineering, I went up to him."

"You were the one who moved the camera away from the stream," Evan murmured.

"He was already out of it by that time," Jenson went on. "All I did was stop a mad man. You should be thanking me."

God, the moron really had lost it. The cops told Vlad to step back then wasted no time restraining Jenson. The moron squirmed like a giant, agitated worm. The cops ordered him to either calm down or he'd be carried to the car and tossed in back. Jenson did as he was told.

Everyone remained silent as the cops borrowed scissors from Zach to cut the tape binding his legs then escorted him to the cruiser. By this point, Jenson looked defeated, as if all of the fight had been drained out of him. Evan started to smile until Corporal Renton arrived. Renton spoke briefly with the officers then wandered up to Evan, Sully, and Cecelia.

"Time to patrol," Vlad said, then disappeared.

Apparently, he still didn't like or trust Renton. Evan didn't blame him. The questions were relentless. By the time Renton was finished and had taken the bag of evidence, Evan was lightheaded and scarcely coherent from being awake nearly twenty hours. He promised to provide a written statement in the morning.

After Sully told Renton about seeing Gardner running down the road, Renton said, "He's been picked up."

"Excellent." Sully turned to Evan. "We did it, dude. Solved a murder in the first forty-eight. How awesome is that?"

"Pretty impressive," Cecelia said, beaming at Evan.

Evan put his arm around her. He was tempted to kiss her but decided to play it cool.

Renton looked from Sully to Evan. "If you were police officers I'd say good work. But you're not. You should have called me when you found the first bit of evidence."

"How could we have told you about the blackmail list without looking guiltier," Sully replied. "Let's face it, you thought we might have done it, right?"

"Not necessarily," Renton replied.

Okeyo Abasi stepped out of HQ, his expression much more relaxed than it had been a few hours ago. "Excellent work, Evan."

"I couldn't have done it without Sully. He found both hiding spots."

"Evan took the big risks," Sully said. "The guy deserves a raise." He turned to Renton. "He also plans to apply for the RCMP next year."

"Let me know when you do," Renton said, "and I'll put a word in for you."

"Thanks." Cecelia gave him a hug. Freakin' amazing.

"Evan's a good decision maker with strong leadership potential," Okeyo said, turning to him. "It seems we have a site supervisory position opening up as of tonight. You should apply."

"I will. Thanks." An endorsement from Okeyo was as good as being offered the position.

"Wow," Cecelia said. "A date, a solved murder, and a promotion all in one evening." She snuggled against him. "You truly are a hero."

"I've been lucky." As long as he got the girl, all was right with the world.

"Way to go, Five-O." Sully slapped him on the back.

"Thanks, man."

The shift supervisors who'd worked here longer than Evan had wouldn't be happy. Too damn bad. After what he'd been through tonight, Evan figured he could handle just about anything. Now that two of the biggest butt-holes on campus were gone, what could possibly go wrong?

~ * ~

If you enjoyed this book, please consider writing a short review and posting it on your favorite review site. Reviews are very helpful to other readers and are greatly appreciated by authors, especially me. When you post a review, drop me an email and let me know and I may feature part of it on my blog/site. Thank you.

Debra

debra_kong@telus.net

Message from the Author

Dear Reader,

I hoped you enjoyed my first novella, *Dead Man Floating*. The character of Evan Dunstan came to me in bits and pieces over a five-year period. He's the kind of person I wished I had worked with while I was in the security field, but alas he is a complete figment of my imagination.

While I was training as a security guard through the Justice Institute of British Columbia, the instructor said that a lot about security could be boring until something happens. And things did happen…a lot. But we also shared many laughs during quieter moments. On that note, I wish to dedicate to this story to the amazing folks I worked with during my time in security. They taught me so much and I'm still in awe of their skill and bravery during really serious situations. Most of all, though, I remember the laughter.

I owe a big thanks to incredibly talented writing friends who gave me invaluable feedback and support while I tackled the novella form. I'd also like to thank Cheryl Tardif for taking a chance on my work. I'm truly grateful for the opportunity to introduce Evan to mystery fans, and to work with such a great team at Imajin.

Cheers,
Debra

About the Author

Debra Purdy Kong's volunteer experiences, criminology diploma, and various jobs, inspired her to write mysteries set in BC's Lower Mainland. Employment as a campus security patrol and communications officer provided the background for her first novella, *Dead Man Floating* as well as her Casey Holland transit security novels, *The Opposite of Dark, Deadly Accusations, Beneath the Bleak New Moon,* and *The Deep End.*

She has also released two white-collar crime mysteries, *Taxed to Death* and *Fatal Encryption.*

Debra has published short stories in a variety of genres as well as personal essays, and articles for publications such as *Chicken Soup for the Bride's Soul, B.C. Parent Magazine,* and *The Vancouver Sun.*

She assists as a facilitator for the Creative Writing Program through Port Moody Recreation, and has presented workshops and talks for organizations that include Mensa and Beta Sigma Phi.

She is a long-time member of Crime Writers of Canada. Look for her blog at http://writetype.blogspot.ca

More information about her books can be found at www.debrapurdykong.com

Debra can also be found on:

Twitter: https://twitter.com/DebraPurdyKong

Facebook: www.facebook.com/debra.purdykong

Goodreads:
www.goodreads.com/author/show/1391841.Debra_Purdy_Kong

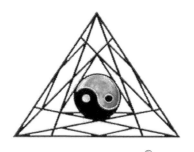

Imajin Books®
Quality fiction beyond your wildest dreams

For your next eBook or paperback purchase,
please visit:

www.imajinbooks.com

www.imajinbooks.blogspot.com

www.twitter.com/imajinbooks

www.facebook.com/imajinbooks

Imajin Qwickies®
www.ImajinQwickies.com

Made in the USA
Charleston, SC
31 January 2017